DYING for KEEPS

AGENTS OF TRAIT

SELESTE DELANEY

Entangled Publishing, LLC
2614 South Timberline Road
Suite 109
Fort Collins, CO 80525
Visit our website at www.entangledpublishing.com.

Ignite is an imprint of Entangled Publishing, LLC.

Edited by Karen Grove
Cover design by Fiona Jayde
Cover art from iStock

Manufactured in the United States of America

First Edition November 2015

ignite

This one is for the Renegades
To paraphrase Malcolm Reynolds:
You keep me believing in the impossible, and that makes you
mighty.
From the bottom of my heart, thank you.

Chapter One

Josh Marron thumped his fist on the desk. "I'm telling you we can't run an op with nothing to go on."

Greta wanted to scream. She'd been hired specifically for her ability to pinpoint trouble. "And I'm telling you something is *wrong*." She started pacing in front of Marron's desk, her hands fluttering. "The missions are off. They have been for a while. Can't you see it? There's no pattern. There *has to be* a structure to it all."

She saw patterns all the time. In everything from sports scores to contrails in the sky. The world, in all its variety, followed certain paths. Things lined up. Most people couldn't see any of it, but Greta couldn't *stop*. It was why this was making her so crazy. The only pattern their recent missions formed was…random. *Nothing* in life was random, no matter how much people wanted it to be. Which meant something was seriously screwed.

"And unless you can tell us where to look for all this

wrongness, my hands are tied. You aren't asking for a mission, Greta. You're asking for an all-out hunt for something you can't define!"

She should have brought Nico with her. He would have convinced Marron to do something. He was amazing with people—all of them as far as she could tell. People weren't her strong suit. She didn't understand how their minds worked or why they couldn't grasp the things she saw so clearly. "How often have I been wrong?"

"Do I need to remind you about the raccoon incident?"

One mistake didn't make her a failure, not by a long shot. She was *not* slacking off, and she certainly wasn't losing her edge. "One time! One." She clenched her hands tightly in an effort to still their motions. "It started with Takamaki," she said, reminding him of the incident where Cal Burrows had to stop an arms deal. "Who in their right mind tries to demo and sell nerve gas at a sci-fi convention?"

"Who ever claimed that asshole was in his right mind?"

This so wasn't the time for jokes. "Fine. Then explain why us, and not the FBI? Or Homeland? Then the ridiculous case Marissa and Trevor were sent on with the Mafia? For a supposedly cursed painting that could change the path of organized crime forever? A *painting*?" She didn't wait for him to retort this time. "Top it off with an attack on our servers and the Senator Carrington mess that Jodi and Finn had to deal with. How can you not see that none of this should have fallen under our purview?"

Marron scrubbed at his face. "Two of those missions were issued directly from Secretary Rickards. He makes sure we have funding. He makes sure we get paid. If he says jump, I'm sure as hell not going to ask if maybe it might be better to have another agency play hopscotch with him instead. When my boss gives us a job, we do it. When I give you a job, you do it. You want to have *any* say in anything, fucking give me some evidence there's a mission to send you on. Otherwise, get the hell out of my office." When she didn't move, he added, "Dismissed, Agent Gallagher." Marron flipped open his laptop and started typing.

Greta blinked. He'd moved past even pretending to coddle her ego, that much was certain. The way his fingers flew over the keyboard implied his entire concentration had shifted to his new task. However, she often had people continue to interrupt her work when she had moved on in similar fashion. Perhaps the dismissal wasn't as final as it seemed. "Sir, I'm not trying to argue—"

"Yes, you are. Now get back to work."

Apparently it was final. Jaw clenched, hands balled, Greta had no choice but to do exactly as he ordered. She stalked to the door and slammed it behind her, the rattling of the glass stretching her already frayed nerves to the breaking point.

He wanted evidence? She'd find it.

Or she'd make it.

Chapter Two

FUCKIN' PERFECT

Nico bolted off the couch when Greta entered the office. Considering the near-purple color of her skin, something had happened while she'd "gone to get coffee." The absence of coffee was also a big tip-off.

"What's going on?"

With the way her entire body shook, she looked like a cartoon character that was literally ready to explode. She tried to open her mouth to speak, but all that came out was, "Arrrggggh!"

Six months ago, he wouldn't have even attempted to touch her, since she ran hot and cold with regard to physical contact. But their time as partners had taught her to accept that Nico wouldn't touch her without cause, and it had taught Nico that platonic touching was the best way to get her to focus and calm down. He ran his hands down her arms, gripping them loosely, just enough for her to notice—just enough for him to want to do more. What he wouldn't give to be able to gather

her in his arms and kiss away whatever worries plagued her. Then again, he wouldn't mind doing that naked, either, feel the soft warmth of her skin pressed to his…

Fulfilling his romantic—or lust-filled—fantasies wasn't on the agenda at the moment though. "Trouble, look at me." When nothing changed, he said it again, adding a little more oomph to the demand. "Look at me."

She did, but she frowned. "That doesn't work on me."

At first he thought she meant the nickname—which he found totally appropriate—then he realized she meant telling her what to do. "I don't know. Considering your eyes are on mine, it kind of looks like it did."

He winked at her and smiled. A return smile wasn't forthcoming, but he'd gotten used to that, too. Smiles were a rare thing from Greta, and he treasured every one. For the moment he had the perfect excuse to stare into her blue-gray eyes and get lost in them.

"I meant that thing you do with your voice. It doesn't work." Yep. That again.

Nico had known for a long time that he had the ability to…convince people of things. He'd always assumed part of it was superior skill at reading others combined with a charming nature. Then he'd met Greta. This wasn't the first time she'd mentioned him doing something with his voice, and he was pretty sure she didn't mean just putting more conviction into his words. Too bad he couldn't figure out what she *did* mean, and she'd been unable to explain it.

"Well, you did what I asked, and you don't have purple skin anymore, so I'm calling non-alien-life-form Greta Gallagher an improvement." She made a face as she always did when he said something silly. Whether or not his *voice* worked on her, she hadn't quite figured him out yet. And that at least put them on an even playing field in one regard. "So, what's going on?"

She waved a hand toward the ceiling, likely indicating the offices upstairs. "Marron. I tried to talk to him about the problem, and he won't listen to reason."

More like he wouldn't listen to ranting.

As much as Nico liked Greta—and he liked her more than he probably should—she struggled to talk to people. Even the amazing eye contact they'd shared earlier was difficult for her. She only fought that battle because she had learned it was necessary.

They'd been working on it for months, ever since he calmly pointed out that when something put her on edge, it was often a miracle if she could string a complete sentence together. She'd been tense when he'd first started working with her at TRAIT, and the stress had only grown over time. He might have worried it was because of him, if not for all the evidence to the contrary.

Namely, the maps and diagrams all over the office. Pins of old missions connected by strings, forming patterns and artistic displays that would be at home in a kindergarten class.

But the artwork wasn't the problem—that was found in the handful of tacks painted red. They connected to nothing. Whenever she had a free minute, she'd try to work them into some other design, find a way to make them fit, but they were always off. One day he'd moved one tack a fraction of an inch to try to get it where it seemed like she needed it. She'd spent the entire day doing calculations and drawings he didn't understand… Until she finally saw the other pinhole.

It was a confrontation he never wanted to repeat. That wasn't the type of closeness he'd hoped to foster with her.

In the end, he learned not to touch her things. While the work she did didn't make any sense to him, it had a clear and undeniable purpose to her.

Sighing, he tore his gaze away from the red thumbtacks and settled it on her again. Much better view anyway. "So, talk to me about what has you so frazzled, and let's see if we can figure out a plan that he'll be able to get on board with."

They'd done this before, but maybe this time something about her process would finally click for him and he'd be able to help her more effectively. He led her to the couch, and they both sat. For a long minute, she didn't say anything, like time had frozen with the two of them here, knees inches apart, holding hands and looking at each other.

Then the warmth of her fingers was gone, and she waved at the maps. "You know my job is to find patterns that signal trouble."

"Yeah. You have something like a ninety-five percent accuracy, too." When he'd been hired at TRAIT, Marron had told him his partner had unique skills. Then he'd watched her and tried to figure out how she did what she did. When that failed, he tried to just figure out what exactly she did, and he couldn't. It was one of those things everyone accepted about Greta. Her mind worked in mysterious and amazing ways, and no one here was going to look that particular gift horse in the mouth.

"Ninety-five plus or minus three percent standard deviation. One failed mission. Stupid raccoon." Her jaw tightened, and he wanted to reach out and run his hand along it, draw her attention away from the past and back to this.

Perfectionist, thy name is Greta Gallagher.

"Let's not worry about that. Talk to me about what's going on now."

"Okay, all these strings…they're patterns of activity. Either ones that led to problems or problems that are patterns in themselves."

He nodded, trying to encourage her. "Like serial killers." He could usually hold on to the idea of her work up until this point. Then she lost him. He really hoped this time would be different.

"Exactly. Nature has patterns. Human behavior has patterns. Computers have patterns. Everything does. Most people can see some of them. I see them all."

Which was clearly both a blessing and a curse.

"And the red tacks?"

"They're assigned missions. Not ones I found, but ones that came from the government. Every once in a while"—she waved toward a map of Montana—"the jobs they give us fit into patterns that were already there, like that weird lab they found outside of Kalispell. And sometimes I find patterns after the fact. But so many of our recent missions...there's nothing."

And...she was losing him. "Couldn't that just mean you haven't found it yet?"

"That's the problem. If there's a hot spot, the pattern is obvious after the fact—even to people without my skills. Because they can look for it. Increased crime in the area. Weird disappearances. *Something* is always off, and when you track those things, they point to the hotspot. But these missions...there's nothing. It's almost like someone dropped bad news on the map like a drip from a jelly doughnut."

He frowned at the maps. Part of him wanted to say that maybe it was just some kind of pattern that she couldn't recognize, some blind spot in her gift. But if that was true, and it only happened with regards to missions that came from higher up the food chain, that was a pattern in itself, and not a good one. Which she would have already figured out.

"You're thinking there's some sort of what? Government conspiracy? They already arrested Attorney General Whiddon after the thing with Senator Carrington's daughter."

She shrugged and looked away from him—a clear sign she was about to say something he wasn't going to like very much. "And why is everyone so very sure she and those thugs who kept attacking Jodi were working alone?"

That was the crux of the problem. And there wasn't a shred of evidence one way or another.

All they had to go on was a bunch of unconnected red thumbtacks.

Fuck.

Greta was glad when they moved from the couch. Sitting there so close had her questioning her sanity. She wanted to touch him more, and that wasn't okay. A long time ago, she'd made a point to clearly delineate the structure of her life.

Family, such as it was, was for casual relationships. These days those consisted of bimonthly phone calls and a visit to drop off gifts on holidays, though she preferred to send a card if she could get away with it. It wasn't that she hated her family or even disliked them. It was simply a matter of them not understanding her and not bothering to try. She left family gatherings feeling rather like the precocious child whose presence is endured at a dinner party rather than enjoyed. So, she simply avoided them whenever possible.

Home was her haven. Now that so many agents were housed in the same complex, it was easy to invite Marissa over for a drink or even to spend an evening discussing *Doctor Who* with Penelope. At home, she had her books and her cat and her solitude whenever she wanted it. At home, she didn't have to worry what anyone thought because she never had people over who would look at her negatively. She and Nico even carpooled to the office more often than not.

But, work was…work. Granted, she was friends with several people at TRAIT, and she wasn't sure she would have survived her first year without Marissa, but work wasn't relaxed in the way she could be at home. There was a separation here, a line that she never came close to crossing.

Except with Nico.

For some reason, they both kept winding up with their toes on that line—and she could never quite place how they ended up there.

Like earlier. He'd held her hands. Why? And why hadn't she noticed it for so long? And after she did notice, why hadn't she wanted to pull away? She knew her boundaries, even if he didn't.

One of the rules about work was no touching unless it was sparring or a life-and-death situation. Business didn't generally require physical contact, especially what she did. But as much as she'd expected him to grow bored and look for a different assignment, Nico was still here, every day, in the basement with her.

And they kept touching.

Not every day or all the time, but often enough to notice. She'd started noticing other things about him, too. Like the way his lips went lopsided when he smiled, and he smiled a lot. The way his brown hair was starting to fall across his forehead now that he no longer had to meet military regulation with regard to length, and how she kept fighting the urge to run her fingers through it.

She shook her head and tried to focus on the computer in front of her. While a distraction from her failed meeting with Marron had been welcome, if she wanted to actually solve the problem, she needed to find a trail to follow. Focusing on random news feeds wasn't going to do her any good—not today.

Instead, she once more brought up the program she'd had Cal create for her. She punched in coordinates: Senator Carrington's home, the site of ConDamned, the hotel in Colorado… All the cases she couldn't account for were logged in. Then she ran scenario after scenario on the map.

After including options to ignore any one or two data points, she was still coming up empty.

She had no idea how long she'd been at it when Nico's hand fell on her shoulder. The weight of it was heavy, comforting, like home. It was yet another feeling that didn't belong here. "Hey, you okay?"

"Of course." Why wouldn't she be?

"Okay. You've just been staring at that map for fifteen minutes without doing anything. That's odd, even for you."

His last words made her cringe inwardly. Different wasn't good—not at work.

But he back-pedaled immediately, as if he knew how much it bothered her. "Sorry. I only meant I know what you do involves periods of looking and thinking. I'm just used to you making noise or…doing something while you're thinking."

"You're used to me?" That implied a level of familiarity she really wasn't sure what to do with—though it probably wasn't how he'd intended it. "I mean used to what I do?"

Nico shrugged like it wasn't a big deal and gave her one of those crooked smiles that made her own lips twitch in response. "We've been working together for six months now. I *am* starting to figure you out." Words failed her, and she simply sat there, blinking at him. Had he actually been trying to understand her all this time? "So, *are* you okay?"

It felt strange to have someone she worked with so closely day in and day out ask something like that. Even Marissa tended to shrug off a lot of Greta's quirks as…quirks. It was easier to focus on the work problem than analyze that any further, even though part of her really wanted to. She waved at the computer screens. "There's nothing new here. I think I'm just frustrated and tired from looking and coming up empty over and over."

"I can see that." He nodded, then reached past her and flicked off the screen. "But it's quitting time now, and you're going to burn yourself out if you spend too much time dwelling on this—at least all at once."

Easy for him to say. He wasn't going to be the one lying awake tonight, trying to connect dots that didn't make a picture. "Going home and putting on slippers sounds like a great idea." Maybe her cat would be in a good mood and snuggle up. Some petting and purring time might wind her down enough so she could sleep.

He pulled her chair away from the desk until she had room to stand. She was reaching for her jacket when he said, "I was thinking maybe on the way to the complex we could stop and grab some takeout."

There were a lot of things Greta had gotten used to while working at TRAIT, including how social some of her fellow agents were during off hours. Gatherings of half a dozen—or more—were all too common. She generally wasn't comfortable with large groups, though, so she avoided the parties whenever possible. As much as she might have enjoyed spending some out-of-the-office time with Nico, she wasn't up to leaving work just to spend time with a bunch of people from work. And the only people she'd known to get together one-on-one were the couples and her girls' nights with Marissa or Pen. Probably better to just ask. "Are you having people over?"

The grin returned, following on the heels of a noncommittal shrug. "I was thinking about throwing in a movie or something."

Noncommittal was as good as a yes. And a movie meant everyone sitting close, talking over the film, and adding to her stress. No thank you. She'd rather be close to Nico when it wasn't such an uncomfortable situation. The fact that she'd rather mix that in with business than a party was something she didn't want to ponder too much. "I'm sure you'll all enjoy that. If you need to stop and pick up food, I don't mind waiting in the car."

Nico's hand was on the doorknob when he turned to look at her once more. "No, I was asking if you wanted to come over?"

"Thank you, but I think I'm going to spend the night with Mr. Perfect instead." For the life of her, she couldn't figure out why that announcement made him look so downtrodden.

Chapter Three

Break In

He'd asked her out last night, and Greta had totally blown him off. At least as much as Greta blew anyone off. After spending the night stewing, he sought out Marissa as soon as he and Greta reached the TRAIT field office in the morning.

Senior agent Marissa Joens was in the middle of discussing tech needs for her next mission with Jodi Israel. He stayed off to the side, watching the women and hoping like hell they would finish up soon. Greta might not miss him in the short term, but the last thing he wanted was for her to decide she wanted him for something and come looking while he was in the midst of this conversation.

Finally, Marissa seemed satisfied, grinning at Jodi as the short redhead made her way down the hallway toward the garage. Then she immediately leaned against the wall, cocked her hip out, and arched a brow at Nico. "Let me guess, I have something you need."

If it had been any other woman, in the same stance,

delivering the same line, he'd have thought it was a come-on. But Marissa was just one of those people who oozed sex appeal like some gave off the garlicky scent of last night's Italian dinner. She couldn't help it. The first few weeks at TRAIT, he'd wondered if she was flirting or not. Then he'd seen Marissa with her husband, Trevor, and realized her normal behavior was *nothing* like she acted with him. The woman was clearly in love and wanted the whole world to know it.

She'd also made it abundantly clear that Greta was her best friend and if Nico did anything to hurt his partner, he'd have to face Marissa's fury. It made her scary in one way but also a key ally in another. He finally nodded and strode toward her. "You do have something I need—advice."

"Uh oh, trouble at Casa Tancredi? Or is it Grotto Gallagher that's the issue?"

"Am I that obvious?" he asked, parking next to her along the wall. Anyone might walk up on them, but this early and this far from the coffee pot, he doubted they needed to fear any eavesdroppers.

"If more people saw you and Greta together, your interest in her would be more apparent, but for now, your secret is fairly safe. I more meant that when people ask for advice, it usually means trouble. Which either means her or your situation with her. You'd be more likely to go to one of the guys for anything else."

And people thought he was perceptive. He didn't have anything on a woman who'd been raised to be a con artist. It was a damn good thing Marron had plucked Marissa out of juvie—the world was far better off with her on their side. "Situation. I asked her out last night, and she kind of ignored the invite."

"Asked her out as in said, 'Greta, would you like to go out on a date with me?' or…"

Nico winced. She'd warned him about this a long time ago. "No. I suggested we stop for takeout and mentioned watching a movie at my place."

Marissa gently banged her head against the wall. "What did I tell you?"

"That I had to be direct with her or she wouldn't get it." He'd thought he'd been as direct as a brick to the back of the head, but obviously not. Then he had a horribly wonderful thought. Greta might be immune to his gift, but her best friend wasn't. "Obviously, I need to work on my delivery. But you know what would really help?"

She latched onto the question like a suicidal fish seeing its last meal dangling from a hook. "What?"

"Since you know how she thinks and how to get the point across, it'd be fantastic if you'd put in a good word for me, let her know I'm interested."

"I can do that, but it won't be right now. I have work to do." She pushed off from the wall. "Catch you later, lover boy."

And, she bit. It was almost too easy to get people to do what he asked when he already knew they *wanted* to help. And it wasn't like he expected Marissa to convince Greta to go out with him, just sort of get her to look at him as something other than her partner and a junior agent. If she wasn't interested… all was fair in love and war and all that, but he was pretty sure they'd never even get to the first-date hurdle much less past it without an outside nudge.

Feeling a lot better about the day, Nico made a side trip to the coffee maker and poured them both a cup. Greta didn't drink much coffee, but he'd found she liked to start the day surrounded by the aroma, and he'd even caught her taking a sip once or twice. One cream. Three sugars. She liked it sweet.

For all the little things he'd learned about her in six months, the one he hadn't broken through yet was how exactly her mind worked. Yesterday had been a step in the right direction. He was hoping today could be another if he played his cards right.

Greta had stopped by Marron's office first thing, planning to talk to him again, but he was on the phone and looked as if he already had a headache. She wasn't going to get anything out of him like that. The basement office she shared with Nico, however, was empty, and only a few minutes staring at the wall had her wishing for noise or any other distraction.

She'd gone back upstairs, planning to hunt for her partner, when she realized she was doing that thing Marissa had spoken to her about when she first arrived. Boundaries.

"Greta, I adore you," Marissa said, with what appeared to be a genuine smile on her face, "but you need to understand that even though I'm your friend, sometimes I need time alone."

"Oh."

Greta had learned over time that Marissa truly hadn't meant anything bad by it, but Greta's tendencies to avoid people disappeared when she found one of her rare kindred spirits. Then she seemed unable to control the need to be around them as much as possible until she burned out from the contact.

Apparently people didn't like that—all too often, it drove them away before she remembered to temper it. And she had started to do that with Nico, hunting him down because he wasn't where he was supposed to be. With her.

She was halfway back down the stairs when she realized he was trailing behind her, carrying two mugs of coffee. Her hand on the rail, she turned and stared him down. She was doing her best to remember personal boundaries and to keep her distance, both emotionally and physically, but it was almost impossible with him this close to her.

"Damn. You caught me. Here I was pretending to bring you coffee so I could accost you in the hall outside the office, and now we're stuck on the stairs." He winked at her, a clear sign the words were a joke.

Nico had started doing that early on in their working relationship. Lately though, Greta found herself struggling with the hints. Her partner's "gift" to the Tactical Response and Investigative Team was his ability to get people to believe anything he said. Or more accurately, get them to believe anything he wanted them to, since he rarely resorted to out and out lying. The main trouble with that skill was it didn't work on Greta, but that hadn't stopped him from trying.

Combined with the winks and nudges, though, she was having a harder time separating fact from fiction. Especially when the conversation hinted at anything personal. Like last night. She'd clearly said *something* wrong since he hadn't stopped for takeout after all, but she never had figured out what.

She needed to do better than that this time. *Humor. This is the time to diffuse the situation with humor.* "And you can't accost me on the stairs? Your skill set seems a bit limited if hallways and offices are the only stage that works for you."

He leaned in close and whispered, "Oh, Trouble, I can handle stairs just fine, but I'd hate to end up burning you with the coffee." Before Greta remembered how to breathe, Nico had edged past her and continued on his path. "One cream, three sugars, just the way you like it."

Greta clutched the railing and watched as he disappeared through the door to her office. Correction: their office. When she'd first been assigned to work with Nico, she'd assumed it was a temporary pairing. After all, his talent was most useful in the field, and she was rarely utilized for field work, considering her difficulties reading people.

But then he'd stuck around.

And she hadn't asked him to leave.

More, she didn't *want* him to leave.

It made no sense. She didn't need him to do her work. In fact, Marron had basically worried at one point that his continued presence hindered her ability to find hot spots of activity for TRAIT to look into. Yet having him around made coming into the office so much more enjoyable. Unlike the other agents, he didn't seem to expect her to bend to his way of thinking, didn't expect her to suddenly understand all the social cues he threw out. He was simply there—with the perfect mug of coffee, with a training schedule that fit both their needs, and with his ridiculous stories.

It didn't hurt that he was easy to look at as well as be around. Exactly six feet tall and broad through the shoulders and chest, he was the perfect size to make her own five-foot-eight seem feminine without making her feel weak. And those arms…she'd never looked forward to sparring until he'd come to TRAIT. Now it was one of her favorite activities.

Even his gift was a point of captivation for her, a riddle to be solved, a mystery unraveled. Other people succumbed to him at every turn—even Marissa, who was a master at manipulation. But not Greta herself.

She wasn't arrogant enough to think it was anything special about her. But what did it say about her connection to Nico? And once she figured it out, what would that mean? Would he become just another coworker? Or was his allure deeper than his good looks and the brilliance of his ability?

The sigh she released was deep but quiet.

Yes, she was attracted to him in ways she didn't fully comprehend. She didn't do attachments—people fascinated her to near obsession until they eventually bored her. One of the reasons she was comfortable with Marissa as a best friend was the knowledge that the former teen con-artist was as leery of personal connections as Greta was. Either of them could bolt at a moment's notice and it wouldn't be unexpected.

A man? That was so far outside her realm of knowledge, she could only assume, at their core, her feelings for Nico were nothing more than carnal urges.

Every so often, she got the sense that he felt the same about her.

Too bad his jokes and winks and playfulness left her completely confused as to whether or not he'd be interested if she approached him about a fling—whether he'd dismiss her completely, or worse, if he'd want something more. And she understood social rules well enough to know if those sorts of advances went badly, it would affect their ability to work together. Well, it would affect his ability to work with her.

Greta had no such problems compartmentalizing messy emotional issues.

Which meant she needed to put Nico into his proper compartment and get back to her job—which, regardless of Marron's concerns, she'd been doing just fine. If their boss would only listen to *her* concerns, maybe she'd be a little less distracted. Though if she didn't find something concrete soon, she might not be able to make any arguments at all. There was a chance Marron would decide she wasn't pulling her weight.

Nico had acted interested in how she pinpointed hotspots. Even yesterday, he'd seemed intent on understanding so he could help her. Maybe she could nudge him today, get them on the same page and working toward the same goal. Then she'd be able to figure out exactly what was going on, get it fixed, and put the world back into nice, predictable order again—before Marron gave her the boot.

Because the last thing she wanted was to be out of a job. Even if a lot of the people here didn't necessarily like her, most of them respected what she did for the team. She loathed trying to find that sort of position again.

And she somehow doubted Nico would follow her if she

had to leave.

It took Greta so long to come into the office, Nico started getting nervous to the point of fiddling with the blinds over the egress window and adjusting the position of the computer monitors. He hadn't done anything vastly different than normal. Coffee, check. Flirting, check. Distance kept at least a centimeter to the safe side of neutral, check.

Tiptoeing around was exhausting, but he didn't want to come on too strong. There was a fine line between direct and asshole. Of course, with Greta, too strong would likely involve showing up in a loincloth, carrying a club, and throwing her over his shoulder. Even that might only get him a calm "What are you doing, Nico?" in response.

Any other woman, and he'd have figured out how to talk to her by now.

Then again, any other woman would have fallen into the webs he wove and proven a complete non-challenge. He'd played that game before. It was boring as hell. Which was a big reason he was drawn to Greta, but it wasn't the only one.

There was nothing boring about talking to her.

The attraction had started before he realized she never fell for any of his stories. Sure, it was interesting to have to deal with that for the first time in…ever. But he'd already been taken in by her ever-changing blue-gray eyes and her dimples. He didn't get to see those nearly as often as he liked, but when she smiled the whole room lit up. And those lips. He'd assumed bee-stung lips were just Hollywood speak for women who got collagen injections—until he met Greta. He'd considered pressing his mouth to hers to see how those lips felt against his too many times to count.

"I thought we'd try something new today." Her voice

startled him so much he almost knocked over her coffee.

"Sounds great. What'd you have in mind?"

"Research. Obviously. We still need to hand Marron a reason to send agents to investigate…whatever is causing all this disruption."

And by that she meant the conspiracy theory she currently had running. Nico didn't want to think she was paranoid, but the more angles he'd examined things from, the more it looked like they were dealing with smoke and mirrors. "Maybe we could see if there's a glitch in the program Cal made. Maybe it's not showing a pattern because of some programming error."

She cocked her head to the side and blinked at him, the light hitting her eyes and making them shift slightly toward blue. "Or we could do research. The program is fine."

Not a fight he could win with the power of suggestion. "Perfect. I'll grab a chair and a notepad."

She booted up her computer and monitors. He'd asked once why she didn't request one of those walls of flat monitors rather than the mishmash that occupied shelves around her desk. Greta had looked at him like it was the most ridiculous suggestion in the world. Apparently there was order in her chaos of monitors, too.

Hooking a foot around a rolling chair, he pulled it forward and took a seat. "Okay, I've watched you do this before, so I'm guessing something different means literally something different."

For a second, Greta paused, her fingers hovering over the keyboard. Then she turned to him, frustration written over all her features. "After how attentive you were yesterday, I'm going to try to explain all of this more clearly, but I don't anticipate you being able to do what I do. It's a unique skill set—like yours."

That was a first. "I've never heard you say that about

what I do."

"Because I've never said it before." The tapping of the keyboard meant she was back at work, the momentary break gone. "I can see the value in tricking people so you get what you want."

Ouch. "Well, it is the spy game. Lying is kind of what we do."

"It's not what I do."

Ouch again. The worst part about her disapproval was, although Greta never fell prey to his suggestions, he knew very well she could be lied to. He'd seen it happen on occasion within these very walls. She couldn't see through the veil of the little white lies people told all the time to make life run smoothly in the same way she could see him twisting a conversation to suit his purposes. So, his skills probably only qualified as "tricking people" because she didn't recognize the other ways in which people did the same thing.

She had an innocence to her that he'd lost a long time ago—the ability to believe in a world of heroes and villains. And to her, heroes told the truth. Not that she would consider him a villain, but she'd see him as…Batman instead of Superman. Flawed.

And he wanted her to see him as better than that.

Nico blew out a breath. *Real.* The only way he'd get inside Greta's defenses was to be totally real with her. He'd recognized it early on, but every so often he needed the reminder. "Okay. Show me what you do and how I can help you."

"I look for patterns, sort of the way Cal can see patterns within codes. I see them within life." Search after search popped up on the monitors.

This wasn't like any type of research he'd seen elsewhere, not even on the most out-there TV shows he watched. "I get Cal's patterns, in theory, but how do you make sense of this mess?"

"For starters, I don't get anything out of the mess. What we're doing now is wandering through the internet, looking for things that are unusual—that don't *seem* to fit. Sometimes a story jumps out at me."

She'd never talked him through this before. He'd always had some other bit of work to do while she'd performed her own personal version of *Where's Waldo*. "So, kind of like the Winchesters search online news stories for things that might be paranormal in origin."

Her hands paused over the keyboard, and her brow wrinkled. "You mean that TV show? *Supernatural*?"

"Exactly." He didn't mention the fact that she reminded him a bit of the angel, Castiel, in the way she interacted with people.

"Perhaps."

Yeah. Vintage Cas. All she needed to do to flesh it out a bit was make some inappropriate comment about the pizza boy. "And how do you figure out that something doesn't fit? I mean, maybe there would be a way for Cal to write another program to save you the hassle of—"

She let out an exasperated sigh, as if he hadn't been paying attention all these months. "There's no math for what I do, and it isn't as simple as vampires and zombies, either. The best way to explain it is that a lot of it is hunches and intuition. I see something, and it triggers a thought process."

"Sorry. I wasn't trying to minimize you to rows of data." He just really didn't know how to help. Waving at one of the screens, he tried again. "So, it's kind of like you're psychic?"

"Are you mocking me? After the *Supernatural* comment, I'm really not sure."

Shit. "No. I'm trying to understand." If it was anyone else, he'd know how to calm the situation, diffuse tempers, but with Greta, all his normal methods flew out the damn window. "If

I tried to explain what you just told me to another person, psychic would be the default assessment."

Greta spun one of the tiny tops that littered the office — something she did whenever she was stressed. "A real psychic can tell you more." She paused and glared at him. "No making fun of me for believing — I've seen some of them work. They get touchy feely with things and can *see* crimes or victims or whatever. I just see connections between events."

As much as he wanted it to make sense, Nico couldn't quite grasp any of it. Except the psychic bit. He'd read enough reports to understand why she believed. "Okay. How about this? While you do your thing, say whatever you're thinking. Maybe if I can see your thought process, it'll help."

"You want me to let you enter the mind of madness?" Her face was a mask of passivity, but she arched a brow at him, and he wasn't sure if she was trying to make a joke or not.

"Since when did I ever call you crazy?"

The top spun again — and another joined it. "Never said it came from you. Fine. Filters off." Clearly, the madness thing hadn't been a joke. She twisted toward the screens and started clicking from one horrible headline to the next.

Unfiltered Greta was exactly what he needed. Once he got a peek inside, maybe he'd know how to talk to her without getting the cold shoulder in return.

They'd been at it all day, barely stopping for lunch and a second cup of coffee for Nico. Greta had to admit, he was picking up on her work better than she'd anticipated. He had good instincts. He didn't have a clue what to do with them in this regard, but he had them.

Unfortunately, it had all been for nothing.

Whether because she couldn't ignore the pins on the wall,

or because Marron's voice kept saying *raccoon* over and over in her head, or because there was legitimately nothing major happening, she couldn't see patterns in anything today. She rubbed at her face, wishing she could view the world the way other people did—without the need for structure and order to everything.

But at least she could see those things. There were other people who needed it but didn't have her ability. She was pretty sure in their shoes, she would be a drooling idiot. As it was, she was just frustrated.

"Maybe we're going about this all wrong." Nico stood and stretched, his spine cracking bit by bit, each noise drawing her attention to him and the way his muscles played beneath the fabric of his shirt. Attractive as the view was, it was just as strange the way a sound like that had started to bring her comfort. It meant she still had a job, still had a partner, and that the day was over.

Blowing out a sigh, she spun one of the tops, hoping that would soothe away a bit more of her tension. "What do you mean?"

Nico shrugged. "We tried doing what you always do, but this *isn't* what you always do. No matter what you say, I know you're looking for a way to make those red tacks into a mission, and that's not your norm, not by a long shot."

He was right. More than right, but she didn't know what to do with the information. There was a way she did things. A structure. It worked. "How am I supposed to do what I do with things that I don't normally do?"

The grin that split Nico's face was lopsided and made her insides turn to something warm and gooey, yet oddly not disgusting. "Well, I'm thinking it's going to involve some out-of-the-box thinking. So pizza will definitely be involved." She groaned at the pun. "And maybe some boxed wine. Or a case of beer."

She rolled her eyes so hard it made her head hurt. "And then?"

"And then, when we're good and drunk, we eat pizza and strategize." He winked and pulled her chair back from the computers. "It always works for Dean Winchester, which means the plan is completely foolproof."

He seemed to have some strange obsession with that show today. But perhaps he was right, a change of scenery and a new tactic might make things fall into place differently, at least in her mind. "I was always more of a Buffy fan, but it's worth a shot." She was pulling on her jacket when a troubling thought hit her. "But if you plan to start drinking right off, we'll be intoxicated by the time food arrives."

"Yeah. And?" He held the office door open for her.

"What is the pizza boy going to think?"

Nico burst into laughter, and for the life of her, Greta couldn't figure out why.

Chapter Four

He'd done it. Granted, he hadn't done exactly what Marissa had recommended, but Greta was at his apartment with her shoes off and a beer in hand. He'd really expected her to be a wine drinker, but apparently she had a thing for microbrews and Stella Artois. When they'd been shopping, she'd clarified the beer rules: Stella was for *drinking* like they planned on tonight, whereas the micros were for *savoring*.

It was like another thousand points in the *Greta is awesome* column.

She had her feet tucked between her bottom and the couch cushion as she glanced around his apartment. It couldn't look that much different from her own. Same building. Same layout. He wondered what she saw—what patterns she'd discerned about him from the décor, or lack thereof. Before he managed to ask, she said, "You have no photos. Not of friends. Not of family."

That so wouldn't have been his guess. "Pics with friends

are on my phone. Pics with family…I guess you'd have to ask my mom."

"She didn't give you any?"

Nico shrugged. Part of him wanted to move away from the topic, but he knew Greta well enough to know she'd feel the urge to dig if he didn't just answer. "I didn't ask for any. Look, it's not a big deal, but when part of coming to TRAIT meant leaving my family behind…it wasn't much of a loss. I was the extra kid—the one who wasn't the star athlete or the scholar or the anything. I was only in the way. When you grow up in that position, leaving it isn't so hard. I just decided to make as clean a break as possible. I don't miss them, and I'm pretty sure they don't even notice I'm gone. It worked out for all of us."

"That's…" For the first time ever, she seemed to be at a true loss for words. While she often spent time thinking silently, it was intentionally so. Now, she bit her lip and looked at her beer, tracing a droplet of condensation with her finger. "I read a book once about a boy who felt a lot like you. The things his mother did to him—"

"It wasn't like that. If there was abuse, it was mental, not physical." He wrapped his fingers around hers, holding on to the beer with her as if it were some sort of lifeline. "Truth is I don't think they were *actively* assholes to me. It was just they weren't ever actively *not* assholes, either. So now I'm a family of one, and I like it that way. I can build my own family from scratch."

Her first response to that was to tip her beer back and take a long swallow. As much as he liked to think it was because his announcement had made her mouth go dry with anticipation of helping him out, he was a lot more realistic than that. Finally, she said, "And how is your plan working so far?"

She was here, wasn't she? He definitely thought things

were finally headed in the right direction—it just wasn't the direction of the bedroom. Yet. "Slow start, but I'm hopeful that, in the end, it'll all be worth it."

By the time the pizza arrived, Greta had a nice buzz going. She didn't normally drink for the purpose of getting drunk, as the lack of control that tended to go with it made her uncomfortable. In this particular case, however, she was more than willing to make an exception. She didn't think it was really possible for her to be more awkward with Nico than she was on a regular basis, and maybe losing a little control would actually help them bridge whatever gap seemed to stand between them.

So far, so good. She even had her shoes off.

Nico had been a wonderful host. They'd talked and laughed. He'd managed to convince her to tell him about how she and Marissa had become friends, bonding over a shared love of all things paranormal, including discussions about the merits of Angel versus Spike.

And every time he smiled, she got warmer and warmer inside. For a brief moment, she'd started to think the beer was the cause of the tingling across her skin. Then she realized it intensified whenever he looked at her a certain way or touched her—no matter how innocently.

She also noticed, to her abject embarrassment, that regardless of where the electricity started, it always traveled straight to her core, until the junction of her legs was throbbing with need.

It was a feeling she hadn't had for years.

A feeling she certainly shouldn't be having in regard to her partner.

She frowned at the beer in her hand. Perhaps the alcohol

wasn't causing the problem, but it certainly couldn't be helping. Maybe she should quit while she was ahead—before she did something stupid.

Nico came in with a box of pizza, plates, and napkins. "Uh…do you want silverware? I usually consider pizza a hands-on food, but I know some people don't."

"Why on earth would people use silverware on pizza? It's designed with a handle. That's just a waste."

"And this is why we work so well together." Laughing, he sat down next to her. Close, so very, very close. "So…red tacks."

Oh, yeah. Work. She'd almost forgotten. "Red tacks."

"I was sort of musing on this at the office, but I couldn't figure out how it would work with your program. Did you ever consider the possibility that it isn't that you have too much data…but that you don't have enough?"

Greta stopped with a slice halfway in her mouth. In order to give herself time to process, she bit and chewed, savoring the spiciness of the meat and the slight crunch of the veggies. Not enough data. Not enough data. "That totally changes… everything."

Nico started talking, but as much as Greta enjoyed the sound of his voice, she barely heard him while her mind began reprocessing the information they had. She knew he tapered off quickly, probably aware she'd gone quiet for a reason. Her program could analyze data and remove it, but without a clearer pattern, how was she supposed to extrapolate what they were missing? Normally they *found* all the data while researching. She dropped her pizza onto the plate and scrubbed at her face.

"It's a great thought. Probably the *right* thought, but I don't know how to use it. Especially if we don't know how much we're missing." Which left them right where they started.

"Hey, Trouble, don't clock out on me yet." Nico moved

closer, wrapping an arm around her shoulders. It was the closest they'd ever been, and the weight and heat of his touch suddenly had her wanting to be closer. "This is a brainstorming session, not have-a-slice-of-pizza-and-an-idea. We can come up with more stuff. We'll jot everything down, and tomorrow, when we're sober, we'll look at all of it again. Maybe we'll find the answer, but maybe we'll have to try some other out-of-the-box thinking."

Out of the box and into the bed thinking?

No. They were coworkers. They had to keep some distance between them. The last thing she wanted—even less than she wanted to go without sex any longer—was to lose him as a partner.

Greta forced herself to glance toward him, planning to thank him for being so great about this and then make some excuse that would put more professional distance between them—whether she wanted to or not. But the way he was looking at her, his gaze soft and hooded, a lazy smile on his lips… Everything about him made her not want to move a single inch.

But if she sat here too long, didn't she risk the body buzz starting again? Didn't she risk slamming right through those few social barriers she'd put up? It didn't matter how many couples there were at TRAIT. Everything she'd ever been taught, everything she'd ever been told, screamed that workplace romances were a bad idea.

But, the beer whispered in her brain, *did it say anything about a workplace kiss? Or even a workplace fling? Those are absolutely, definitely, not the same thing. At all.*

Just as she vowed to switch to water, Nico cracked open another Stella and handed it to her.

Right. The plan. The map. The missions without a pattern.

Risks. Too many risks. She either risked being inappropriate with her partner, or she risked national security—and who knew how many lives—if she missed an answer because she didn't embrace this weird, albeit already fruitful, tactic that was also having the unexpected effect of firing up her libido.

She stared at the beer for a long minute, and then Nico said, "What if it's not all pointing at one thing, either? What if we have a couple of separate issues that are causing all these anomalies of yours? We've only looked for a pattern that put them in one big group."

Another good thought.

Damn it. For God and country. Or at least country.

The beer bottle tipped toward the ceiling, and crisp, cold ale washed down her throat. She only hoped she didn't regret it come morning.

Nico really hadn't been intending to get Greta *drunk*. She seemed to hold her liquor really well early on, and they hadn't even eaten at that point. Considering the number of women he knew who could keep up with, and even outdrink him, he figured she was safe so long as she acted normal. Besides, it wasn't like she'd be driving home, what with living the next building over. And he had no plans to take advantage of her.

This was just an initial semi-social thing outside of the office.

Even if they were still working.

It was a first step; that was all. And like he'd told her, he felt pretty good about the plan to take things slowly. Just not…sloth speed. Or snail speed. Or even tortoise speed. He was hoping for more of a meandering horse from an old spaghetti western.

But at least she'd liked the ideas he came up with.

Turned out Greta's thinking outside the box was a lot more…outside the realm of physics. But that might have been the beer talking. It was hard to tell sometimes.

"What if the points aren't making a pattern because it has nothing to do with any pattern we know here on earth because it's extraterrestrial in nature?" She raised a finger and nodded like she'd just made the world's most sage announcement.

"Trouble, I think you're drunk."

"No. I'm just smarter than you."

He would have argued, but she *was* smarter than him. So he let it go, after all, he couldn't prove the nonexistence of aliens, and for all he knew, she had secret intel on Area 51.

Then, about an hour later, she said, "Then again, what if it's dragons? There could be some tunnel running through all those points, but because we don't know about dragon hibernation tunnels, I can't make sense of it. Never mind that they'd probably be like ants and go deep, too. That adds another dimension to the pattern." She started giggling at the atrocious pun.

Definitely drunk. No matter what she said, it was time to get her home. Nico made a point of exaggerating the gesture when he looked at his phone. "Damn. It's midnight already. We should probably pack it in and look this over in the morning."

Greta waved at the paper in front of him as she put on her shoes. "You wrote it all down?"

"I did." *Even the aliens and the dragons.*

"Okay." The minute she stood, he realized she had blown by tipsy a *long* time ago. His arm was around her waist before she fell. It felt far too good to have her body pressed tight to his like this—at least far too good for meandering horse speed. "You're fast."

If he'd been fast, he would have caught on to her intoxication earlier. Now he just needed to get her to her place. At his door, he picked up her purse, keys, and jacket in his free hand. Fortunately it was a warm enough evening the jacket wasn't really a necessity to hop from one building to the next. The security door clanged shut behind them, and Nico kept a steady grip on his partner as they crossed over the damp grass. Unlocking and opening the other security door was more of a hassle. Considering how heavy the steel was, he almost lost Greta trying to swing it wide enough to get inside.

Beer may have been a bad idea.

Once they were in the hallway, though, he wished he'd just suggested she pass out in his guest room.

Marissa stood in her own doorway, arms crossed, foot tapping. "Fun night?"

"Marissa!" Greta practically launched herself at her friend. "We got so much done. Did you know he's pretty smart when he's not at work? Can you tell Marron to put a keg in with the coffee machine? It might up productivity." She slurred and staggered over half the words, but for the most part, she still sounded better than he'd expected.

Nico gave a half-hearted smile. "I really thought she was okay."

"I'm fine." Greta dragged the word out for at least three seconds.

Marissa just frowned. "I'll open her door and get her to bed."

Nico handed her the keys, and she led the way down the hall to the next door. As she twisted the key, he asked, "What are you still doing up anyway?"

Her shrug was an odd combination of nonchalant, dismissive, and tense. "I was keeping an eye on a strange vehicle in the lot. Heavily tinted windows, looks fairly shady. I've seen it before. Probably just someone visiting a friend, but after what happened with Jodi and Finn…"

She referred to the attacks in the spring, tied to one of

Greta's red tacks. A chill raced over Nico's skin. "Yeah. Probably."

"Anyway, I saw the two of you coming in and figured you might need a hand. The car hasn't moved in an hour. No one in or out." Marissa popped open Greta's door and held it, waiting on them but not really paying attention. Like she was giving them a private moment.

It was only then Nico realized she thought it was what he'd asked her about earlier—a real date. Shit. She was never going to stop giving him grief about this. His fingers tightened on Greta's side briefly, and she giggled, half twisting out of his embrace. He reached for her waist just as she drunkenly grabbed him by the neck.

He didn't know if she'd fallen against the wall and pulled him down or if she'd yanked him closer on purpose. All Nico knew for certain was Greta's mouth was pressed to his, and it was everything he'd imagined and more. Her lips were like silk, and then her tongue traced the seam of his mouth, and he bit back a groan.

Of all the times to stumble on Marissa in the hall. He wished like hell she wasn't watching, but she was. Besides, he'd promised himself not to push Greta at all, so he eased away from the kiss slowly, fighting the urge to move back in for just one more minute, one more second. Only when he was standing well away from her did he swallow and force out the words, "Get a good night's sleep. We have a lot of work to do tomorrow."

But Greta didn't hear him; she was borderline passed out against the wall as Marissa led her stumbling into her apartment.

At least he didn't have to deal with a lecture from Marissa tonight. That was just about the only plus he could see. He dropped Greta's purse onto the table just inside her apartment and draped her jacket over it. After closing her door, he spun around. Time to make a hasty exit before Marissa finished up and he got stuck talking to her. He'd much rather revel in the very drunken but very real kiss.

Too bad when he stepped outside, he noticed the SUV Marissa had mentioned. It gleamed black under the parking lot lights. That, coupled with the dark windows, made it stand out almost as much as a blazing red sports car.

He realized he'd been staring at it for a long minute, which was beyond stupid, and was about to go to his own building when the headlights flared to life. Momentarily blinded, he turned away. But this was no resident from one of the buildings using an automatic starter to warm up their ride before they came out to leave. The engine immediately roared, and the thing sped off into the dark. Someone had been sitting there, watching Nico as he watched the car.

Maybe Greta needed to put another red thumbtack on Naperville.

And maybe, just maybe, moving so many agents into the same building had been a really bad idea.

Chapter Five

Greta woke up with a headache and a tongue coated with fuzz. Or at least it felt like it was. After brushing her teeth and tongue three times, she chugged a glass of water and a few ibuprofen.

I kissed Nico.

The thought raced through her skull as she twisted on the shower and let steam fill the bathroom. She'd woken up to a note from Marissa that had filled her in on the end of last night—in case she didn't remember. Now she was wondering if it would have been better if she'd been able to pretend it had all been a dream. Fantasizing about coworkers, while probably not a good idea, wasn't anywhere near on the same level of verboten as kissing one.

But he kissed me back.

The problem was…that was all she remembered, that the kiss had happened. If Marissa had stayed, Greta wouldn't have been able to tell her if it was a good kiss, a bad kiss, if tongue had been involved. Nothing. She had the intellectual knowledge that their lips had pressed together and moved, and that was it. Not that Greta had much experience in such things, but it seemed as if her first impulsive, drunken kiss had been an utter fail.

What if he doesn't remember it at all? What if it was bad?

She'd wind up looking at him, trying to remember what his lips felt like, and he'd wonder why she was staring. Or worse.

This was going to be an utter disaster. How was she supposed to work with him day in and day out, not knowing what that one foolish moment had done to their partnership? And she was supposed to drive to the office with him.

Oh no. Not today.

She rushed through her shower, no longer caring about the pounding in her head. It would go away with hydration and time. As she dried off, Mr. Perfect mewled, twining in and out of her legs, clearly unhappy about being left alone for so long yesterday. Food and fresh water in their appropriate dishes seemed to appease the irritated tabby enough for Greta to get back to her morning rush. After running a comb through her unruly waves, she slicked on some cherry ChapStick, threw on clothes, and ran next door to Marissa's.

Her friend answered on the first knock. "What's up, panic-monkey?"

"I am not panicking." Greta shifted as Marissa arched a brow at her. "Okay, fine. I might be a little frantic this morning. Can I get a ride to work with you?"

"Are you okay? I assumed you would be happy about what happened."

"He's my *partner*."

"And Trevor's mine. I *know* you got full details on our fake honeymoon."

"And on your real one. But I'm not you." Her situation

was totally different from a mission gone sideways that led to a fake engagement becoming a real engagement. She was just…disobeying the rules. She didn't do that. Not without a damn good reason, and her libido was a lousy reason.

Marissa was still staring, and every minute they stayed here was more time for Nico to finish getting ready and show up to take her to the office. "It's complicated. It doesn't matter if I'm attracted to Nico. I can't focus on work if I'm distracted with thoughts of him. I can't do my job, and if I can't do my job, eventually I'll be out of a job. And then—"

Marissa cut her off with a finger to her lips. "Got it. Not panicking at all. Trevor already went in with Cal to grab a workout. So I'll get my keys and purse, and we can go."

"Okay. I'll wait here." The snort that escaped her friend was accompanied by choked back laughter. "What?"

"Just thinking you might want to put on a bra and shoes before we take off. But I suppose this might be your attempt to give casual-Fridays a new twist."

Greta looked down. She had indeed forgotten a significant portion of her clothes. It only took a minute to race back to her apartment and remedy the situation, but it was one more sign she didn't have any clue how to deal with today. As soon as she and Marissa were in the car and away from the complex, Greta texted Nico.

CAUGHT AN EARLY RIDE TO THE OFFICE. WANTED TO GET STARTED ON SOME OF THE IDEAS YOU CAME UP WITH.

He texted back less than a minute later.

OH. OKAY. I WAS JUST ABOUT TO WALK OVER TO YOUR PLACE. GUESS I'LL SEE YOU AT WORK.

"Let him down easy?" Marissa drove without looking at Greta.

"I didn't let him down at all. I simply told him I was riding with you."

"Yeah…and I'm sure that didn't seem strange at all. You

need to figure out your shit before he gets to the office. You know that, right? This isn't all about your distractions. Nico has a stake in this, too."

Her shit. Marissa never minced words. It was something Greta both loved and hated about her. But she was right; Greta cared about Nico, and the last thing she wanted was to mess up what they already had. Even if a part of her couldn't stop wanting more. "What am I supposed to do? It never should have happened. And it never *would* have happened if I hadn't gone over there last night."

The sigh from behind the steering wheel was so deep, it sounded as if Marissa was in mourning. "That's up to you, but you can't leave him hanging, wondering what's going on. Move forward or shut it down, but you can't just pretend it didn't happen, because I guarantee he was sober enough to remember."

The kicker was that a big part of Greta wished she'd been that sober, too.

Then again if she had been, the kiss probably wouldn't have happened.

And she had no clue if that would be better or worse than where she found herself right now.

Nico pulled into a slot in front of the TRAIT office and threw his car into park. Today was going to suck ass. Greta was clearly in avoidance mode, which meant instead of last night being a stepping stone, it was a train wreck. Then there was the strange SUV in the apartment lot. It hadn't been back this morning, but he'd lost a lot of sleep dwelling on it last night.

No one had gotten into the vehicle the whole time he'd stared at it. So, whoever was inside had been sitting there a while. Marissa had said no one got in or out while she'd kept an eye on it from her apartment window. But there'd been a gap between her watching the SUV and him stepping outside and noticing it.

Someone could have easily walked outside and climbed into the thing while they'd been in the hallway working to get Greta into her apartment. The only problem with that scenario was Nico had watched the SUV for a while before the lights came on. How many people hung out in parking lots late at night like that?

It was probably nothing, but he didn't want to ignore the possibility of trouble.

He stepped into the gray building and passed by Sara, their receptionist in the lobby, giving her a nod in greeting. Really she was an agent, but they needed to put on a front in case anyone walked into the building looking for a different office or a public restroom.

At one point he'd wondered how she'd gotten stuck with the gig, but someone had mentioned that she was a "retired" NSA agent. Considering her smile always seemed to hold a hint of threat in it, Nico never bothered asking why she retired. Cats could keep their curiosity. Nico preferred to live.

Blowing past other agents and even the coffee machine, he beelined straight to Marron's office. The door was open, so he walked right inside. Just in time to hear Marron say, "Of course, Mr. Secretary, but you're putting us on a budget the local PD couldn't work with. I'm not sure what you expect me to do." A long pause. "Yes, I do understand." Then he clicked off the phone, looking like he was about to chuck the handset across the room.

"Bad news?"

Marron slid the handset calmly back in the cradle. "That obvious?"

Nico debated pushing for details, but it was pretty clear

from what little he'd heard. Secretary of Defense Rickards was cutting their budget…again. "Yeah. Pretty obvious. What can we do?"

"You can all get second jobs and do this one for free." Marron scrubbed at his face. "I'm guessing you didn't come in here to discuss budget woes, though. And if it's about Greta's mission to nowhere, as you can tell, it's not an option."

Which wasn't something he planned to tell his partner—they had enough things to deal with today without him confirming that their boss still said no. "After I tell you why I'm here, you might re-think that."

Marron waved him toward a chair. "Hit me."

"There was a strange SUV in the apartment lot last night. Marissa was watching it for a while, and when I walked outside and saw which one she was talking about, it took off."

Eyes narrowing, Marron said, "That story sounds like it's missing a lot of details. Fill in the blanks, and none of your special skills."

Not that he'd have cause to use his gift, but he wasn't about to say he and Greta had gotten drunk and made out, no matter how much he'd enjoy reliving the memory. "Greta and I worked through dinner—pretty late actually, and I walked her to her place. Marissa came out to talk to her and mentioned the vehicle, said it had been around before. When I left the two of them, I went outside and was staring at the car, trying to figure out if it was trouble or not. After a few minutes, it drove away."

"And you're concerned it could be something like the attack on Jodi and Finn last year?"

"Maybe? I don't really know. It just seemed out of place enough to mention."

Marron scooted his chair away from the desk, stood, and started perusing the books lining his shelf. "Let me get this straight. You thought there might be trouble, so you went out and stared it down, alone. At least tell me you were armed."

Nico hadn't even needed to hear the words. He'd known when Marron turned around that he was in trouble. The avoidance was the way the head of TRAIT gathered his composure before tearing someone a new one. "I thought there was a strange vehicle in the lot and figured being able to describe it might prove helpful."

"Fine. Describe it." Marron sat back down and started taking notes. When Nico was done, he said, "Plates?"

"None on the front, and I couldn't make out the back. So either it was out of state or they'd removed the plates." Either was a distinct possibility since the exhaust fumes had concealed where the rear plates would have been.

Marron let out a sigh. "Okay. Since we haven't had any more firewall problems, and there's no direct threat, I'll send out a memo. Alert everyone so they keep an eye out, but start being a little more careful."

"Will do."

"And get Greta back on track. If we want our budget restored, we need to start showing Rickards some goddamned results."

"On that, too." Nico spun on his heel and left the office. The budget thing felt like an itch in his brain, one he couldn't quite scratch. One of the first things he'd done after coming to TRAIT was read through old mission files.

While there was a lot redacted, they had a solid track record. Even so-called "failed" missions weren't really failures—they just hadn't been perfectly successful. An arms dealer set off a toxin on US soil, but the gas had been vented and all the people involved captured. A painting had burned, but the Mafia don who had been the source of the trouble had been brought down in the scuffle. Armed mercenaries had broken into a senator's house but had been stopped before kidnapping the guy's daughter.

Those were the bigger mishaps. All of them were repre-
sented by red thumbtacks on Greta's map, but none were failures in the purest sense of the word.

So why was their funding doing a disappearing act? And
why the hell did they need to *prove* themselves? The only true
failure of a mission had been the one that marred Greta's
perfect record. Neighborhood in Arlington called Aurora
Heights. She'd been certain there was something there, but
when they arrived, all they'd found was a rabid raccoon that
animal control captured and put down.

To this day, she insisted there was something more. Nico
was starting to wonder if she wasn't right.

Who was he kidding? Greta was always right, or at least
always on the right track.

He made his way downstairs, determined to do everything
he could to get TRAIT back to where it should be—the best,
if most secret, intelligence agency in the country. And that
meant making sure Greta figured out her mystery—one way
or the other—so she could get back to work.

Opening the door to their office, he said, "How do you
want to prioritize our list of possibilities?"

Before he knew what was happening, the door slammed
behind him and Greta said, "Right now there is a different
priority." Then her mouth was pressed against his, and he forgot all the reasons it was so damned important to work while
they were in the building.

Nico's lips moved under hers, and Greta melted. Her mind
might not have remembered what this felt like but her
body certainly did. She melded against him. Hip to hip. Chest
to chest. Flesh on flesh. In that moment, nothing other than
the two of them mattered.

A sudden image of them naked and doing more than kissing flashed through her brain, and panic overtook the pleasure of the kiss. No, no, no, no, no…

Kissing was one thing. That was too much.

He must have felt her pulling back mentally from the kiss, because he took a physical step away. "Greta…"

All she wanted was to pull him close again, to feel the heat of his touch, the pounding of his heart next to hers. She shouldn't have kissed him. Marissa had told her to move forward or put the brakes on permanently, and instead she'd only made things even more complicated.

Part of her wished they'd met at the grocery store. Then things could have progressed normally, without their partnership looming overhead like a ticking time bomb.

But it never would have happened. She wouldn't have spoken to him at the store, much less anything else. If they hadn't met here and become partners, she'd still be in her basement office with nothing but her tops and computer monitors to keep her company.

The thought of never having him in her life clawed at her, hurting her in ways no one ever had before. There'd been a hollow in her that she'd never even noticed before he arrived. Now it was filled. If he left… Her stomach twisted, and she wrapped an arm around herself. She needed Nico, and she'd just chosen to put everything they had at risk. No more. She needed to stop things before she made them worse.

"We should work." In a rush, she was back at her desk, scooting toward the keyboard.

"We should talk about this."

He'd done it again. Pushed that tone into his voice. She knew he didn't do it consciously, but it grated on her, poking at every button that made her want to get confrontational. And snapping would be so easy. It would be a release for all the emotions she didn't know how to deal with, but she'd done enough damage. "No. We have a job to do. We're at work. We do our job here."

"Fine."

It wasn't, though. The disappointment in his voice was clear enough anyone would have heard it, but for Greta it echoed, dancing around in her brain with Marissa's warning. She'd done this to him. Not once, but twice. When Marissa had said she needed to make a decision, she'd thought kissing him again would get him out of her system and her out of his—if she'd been there at all. Instead, it only made her want him more.

She had to focus. They'd figure out the rest later. Somehow. Maybe.

Blowing out a breath filled with regret for putting him second, for putting herself second, she pulled up the data points again. "First item on the list?"

"If we start at the top, it's that we're missing data points rather than having extras. If we start at the bottom, it's dragons and the tunnels they burrowed underground."

Greta winced. She must have been really drunk. While she didn't discount the possibility of dragons having existed at some point, she wasn't prone to flights of fancy when dealing with real-world problems. "Let's start at the top then." There was a way to put "empty" data points into the program, but it still relied on having the right number of points total. "How many do you think we might be missing?"

"Run it with one, and let's see what happens."

She punched in the code and let the computer do its thing. Nothing. She shook her head. "Trying again with two." This time, dozens of possibilities popped up that would send them all over the country. "Great," she groaned. "Now I can tell Marron we think we narrowed down the possible trouble zones from everywhere to about forty-five hot spots in thirty different states."

Nico leaned over her, one hand on the desk, the other

braced on the back of her chair, his fingers close enough to touch her if only she leaned back a little. It took every ounce of her self control to stay still. "Something's been bugging me lately. Are you willing to test a conspiracy theory?"

That was the second time in as many days that he'd used the term. Her desperate mind grabbed onto it like a drowning person clutched at a life preserver. "What?"

He didn't look at her, his eyes stayed glued to the screens. "Put in DC as one of the missing points. Can you do that?"

"All of DC? The system works best if we have an exact location like Senator Carrington's house or something."

He tapped his fingers on the desk, eyes narrowing, brows pulling together. The total concentration on his face made her wonder what else he might like to focus all his attention on if given the chance. The thought made heat rush to her core. The fantasy was shattered when he said, "Not DC then. Put in the coordinates from the raccoon. Put in Aurora Heights. Then explain to me exactly how you targeted that area for a mission."

That was infinitely more precise than the District of Columbia. And it meant he was willing to believe she hadn't screwed up with that mission. Considering how many government employees lived in Aurora Heights, it fit with the conspiracy thing, too.

Greta pulled up the longitude and latitude for the center of the neighborhood. While more specific was better, that should be near enough for the system. With it typed in, along with one blank data point, they waited.

"I'd been noticing strange things around several key locations. The security system at the White House went dark for no discernible reason. It was back up in seconds, but normally something like that is the sign of an impending hit. Nothing ever happened—and I made sure to check other agencies. Then there was weirdness at the Naval Observatory.

A few other areas as well." She pointed at the map. All the pins for that mission were black, as was the tack on Aurora Heights.

Nico frowned as he studied the pins. "President at the White House. VP at number one Observatory Circle." He pointed at one of the other pins. "Isn't this where the Speaker of the House keeps his home office?"

Greta stood and pointed at the other pins in turn. "And the Secretary of the Treasury. And the Secretary of State. And then we're back at Senator Carrington's place again. I'd planned to hunt to see if there were issues with other cabinet members, but so many of them live in or around Aurora Heights anyway, that when the program spit that out as an answer, I took it to Marron. But all we found was the damn raccoon—and the area's been silent ever since."

Nico scrubbed at his face, studying the map. There was no way he could know how much his faith in her meant, especially after everyone in the office had dismissed the mission as a fluke. Like that was supposed to make her feel better. She wanted to thank him, but after what she'd done earlier, she didn't know how to find the right words.

Then the computer bleeped, signaling her that the program had finished running.

As soon as the image came on the screen, Greta's mouth went dry. There was only one possibility this time.

This was it. Nico was right. *She was right.*

She wasn't sure why she was so certain, but she *knew* they'd found the right pattern.

Nico punched a finger at the screen, at their missing data point: roughly twenty-five degrees north, seventy degrees west. "There. We need to find out what's there."

"The ocean. A whole lot of Atlantic Ocean." But Greta could find out what else was there. Somehow it felt like the future for her, for TRAIT, for…everything might depend on it.

Chapter Six

Outta My Head

They had a place; they only needed evidence. That should be easy enough. The problem was, searching at sea wasn't going to get her much to take to Marron. And she certainly couldn't take him a conspiracy theory that included the damn raccoon. She needed to focus on information on land—specifically US land—which made things a bit trickier.

Her gaze roved over headline after headline. When nothing sparked, she grabbed two of her tops and started them spinning.

Nico was by her side less than ten seconds later. "What's wrong?"

"There's nothing going on anywhere around there. Nothing at all."

His fingers tapped on the desktop, one of them bumping a top. It stuttered to a stop. "There's nothing going on *now*. But the raccoon was shortly after the incident at Senator Carrington's, right?"

"Yes. I thought maybe there were more people involved, like I mentioned earlier."

"Okay. So, what if you backtrack? We know it's related to the raccoon, but it's also related to missions going back as far as…what? Summer of 2013?"

He was right. Just because there was nothing happening now, didn't mean nothing had happened in that window. Greta tapped on her keyboard, making her system run searches backward through time. "If this gets us anything, I owe you."

"I'll happily take payment in the form of conversation and maybe another kiss."

She thought about retorting, but she'd promised herself to stick to work while in the office. It was the only way she knew to get through this confusion. Of course, he hadn't made that easy.

Another kiss. She couldn't think about that, not if she wanted to focus. When she reached for one of her spinning tops again, she jerked her hand back, pulling it tight against her. Nico had noticed last time she spun them. She needed some space right now. Tops were clearly a no-no. The next thing she knew, her pinky was in her mouth. Not sucking or chewing on it, she just held it between her teeth—a surefire way to keep from doing anything weird.

Though he'd obviously paid attention, Nico had never questioned her collection of tops or how often she played with them, but she didn't want him to start now. And being this close to the answer for all her worry over the last several months had her terribly on edge. With him hovering over her shoulder, watching how she worked, everything was going to stand out.

If she planned to put a stop to their…whatever, his attention shouldn't matter. It did, though, which only made her more nervous, wondering what it meant to her plan to keep her distance. Of course, distance was relative with the way the heat of his body and breath were warming her neck, making her think of other ways he could warm her even more.

She shook off the thoughts and forced herself to focus on her computer.

The words on screen turned into a blur of tragedy, violence, and hatred. So many horrible things in the world — but none of it was what she was looking for.

Then, from a year and a half earlier, a headline practically screamed at her, begging for attention. *New Beach Menace.* On its own it wasn't that different from any other story, but the lead told her otherwise. *A pair of bottle-nosed dolphins washed onto the shore south of Miami, carcasses bloody as if chewed upon. Shark attack feared, swimmers warned to stay close to shore.*

"That's not good." With fingers that felt like they'd frozen in the last several seconds, she cleared the rest of the windows and refocused her search around the Miami area at that time. *Please don't let there be more. Please.* But at the same time she wished it, she needed there to be more.

"Okay. But why did that one stick out to you?" Nico asked, pointing at the screen with the dolphin article. "There were other bad things that popped up during your search, too. Some a lot worse than sharks."

Greta trembled as she clicked on another news story, one that happened a little farther south, two days later. *Amber alert: Michelle and Patrick Thompson. Last seen leaving Deerfield Park Elementary yesterday. Local police are looking for any information…* She swept the article onto another screen.

"I just know it's wrong." That wouldn't be enough for Nico, though. She did her best to explain. "If I believed it was really a shark issue, I'd agree with you. But if a shark managed to injure a dolphin badly enough that it — and its mate — would wash up on shore, it would have eaten one or both of them.

Dolphins are known to survive shark attacks on a regular basis. It's estimated that upwards of two-thirds of bottle-nosed dolphins have healed shark bites. *One* being attacked this badly would be odd. Two? That says this isn't a shark, or not a normal one. So it's a combination of information and instinct."

West Palm Beach fishing charter presumed lost at sea. Bride-to-be still holding vigil, waiting for fiancé and his friends to return.

Homeless man shot. In the midst of a violent killing spree, a homeless man was shot and killed by police. Evidence points to another case of bath salt overdose.

Bad. Bad, bad, bad… So much bad, all in the space of a couple weeks. Those articles filled another monitor.

"Trouble? What's wrong?"

She heard Nico's voice like it was buzzing around her head—a noise she couldn't shut off but couldn't pay heed to, either. As she widened her search, article after article only served to make the location burrow into her brain deeper and deeper until there wasn't anything else. Cuba. Haiti. The Dominican Republic…

"Greta!"

Her chair spun away from the computer monitors, and she found her face only inches from Nico's, too close to ignore. Too close not to notice the hint of stubble along his jaw or the depth of his dark brown eyes. Or the way his brows pulled together. Worry. He was worried. That was why his hands were on her arms. Why he'd turned her away from the monitors and her work.

His grip curled around her wrist. "Let go."

It was only then she noticed the pain in her finger. She opened her mouth, and he tugged her hand free. Her teeth had left more than imprints behind this time; blood pooled in the shallow cuts she'd made. "That doesn't usually happen."

"I know. Because you usually play with your tops when you concentrate. Let's get you bandaged up." He tried to tug her from the chair.

He wasn't supposed to know that—it was closer than she liked people to get. Closer than she was supposed to let him get.

Shaking her head, she twisted back toward the monitors. "We need to print this all out first."

"You can do that later. What you really want now is to avoid staining your blouse."

Greta blinked. His voice had changed, dropped into the lower register he used when he made people listen to him. He was worried enough to try that even though he knew it didn't work. Something bloomed in her chest, a rush of emotion so strong it stole her breath for a second. Focusing on that wasn't an option, though.

She shook her head in response to him. "Stop trying to distract me. If you're that concerned, find a med kit while I print this."

His fists clenched at the edge of her vision—frustration, not rage—then he let out a sigh and stalked out of the room. He'd forgive her for shooing him out. He forgave her for everything else.

Besides, she needed the breathing room right now. Beyond how unnerved she was that Nico had very obviously noticed her fidgeting with her tops—noticed her tells—they were going to take this to Marron soon, and she needed to not be frantic with worry. He wouldn't respond to that at all. She needed to calm the hell down; this was the time to have data and a plan.

She plotted the locations of the news stories on the computer. A map of Florida came up, displaying them, but it didn't see the pattern. She did, though. It was there, a near perfect arc. She zoomed out and printed the page. Using her compass tool, she connected the locations, then completed the circle, the line taking her path far out into the Atlantic.

The instant she moved to put her finger back in her mouth, it throbbed with pain, and she gripped her favorite top—the *Buffy* one Marissa had bought her when they'd first become friends; it had Mr. Pointy chasing a set of bloody fangs when it spun. *Calm down, Greta. Make sure it's there.* She closed her eyes and let the top spin; the sound of it whirring against her desk soothed her nerves. Looking at the map once more, she swallowed hard.

The top wobbled and clattered to a stop.

The point where the compass punctured the paper was almost exactly twenty-five degrees north, seventy degrees west. Exactly where the pattern they'd found said it would be. Something was definitely out there.

Injury forgotten once more, Greta sucked in a deep breath. Whatever else it might be, there was no way in hell Marron could pretend a raccoon was causing issues in the Atlantic waters.

Nico dabbed antiseptic on Greta's injury, savoring the contact even as he tried not to worry. Why had she done that? She had her tops all over the place; she should have been fine.

Was it just the pressure of this discovery? Or did it have to do with last night and then the kiss earlier? She hadn't mentioned either incident—he probably shouldn't, either, no matter how much he wanted to. Tipping his head toward the printer and the stack of paper spewing out, he said, "What now?"

"Now we talk to Marron." Nico barely had Greta's finger bandaged before she was out the door with her stack of printouts. She barged up the stairs and into Marron's office like she owned the place, then slapped the stack of paper on his desk.

"Knocking. It's called knocking, Gallagher." Marron's glare shifted from Greta to Nico.

Like he could have stopped her. Nico just shrugged—there was no right answer, and he wasn't going to try to get them out of trouble until Greta had said what she came here for.

"Knocking is for houses, bedrooms, and single-stall bathrooms. My boss, alone in his office during working hours when I have an emergency, doesn't require it." She shoved the papers toward him. "We need a team in Miami, Florida."

Sighing, Marron scrubbed at his face. He didn't say anything until after he swept his hands through hair going prematurely salt-and-pepper gray. "With all the budget crap hanging over our heads, I can't send a bunch of people anywhere without damn good reason, and one of your hunches isn't enough. Especially not after the last one. So this better be good."

"But…it's a circle!" She stabbed a finger at the map. "Circles are worse than lines. Circles mean setting up shop. It means if we're finally getting wind of it, it might be too late. It—" She clamped her lips together, and Nico watched as she forced herself to stop ranting. And he knew she couldn't tell Marron the one thing that mattered most, the thing no agent should give voice to—this one scared her. He wanted to touch her, to hold her hand. Anything to give her support, but the best way to do that was to talk to Marron—make him see reason.

"Look, Greta, I can't send a team. Not until this budget crisis is over." Marron stood and came around the desk, reaching out like he might touch her. That wouldn't go over well. She was frazzled; more than that, she saw their boss as the enemy right now.

Nico moved to intercept, but it was too late.

"I don't need a hug; I need a team. In Miami."

With the way Marron's jaw clenched, maybe Greta did need Nico after all. He stepped forward, putting himself marginally between her and their boss. "Look, you told Greta to teach me about this stuff, and you said to find a mission. She did. I watched her figure this out, but that's like learning how to be a spy in a classroom. You know?"

Marron grunted. The guy was a strong believer that people didn't learn anything until they were in the field. Nico just needed to play on that, and they'd be golden.

Finally Marron rounded his desk and sat down again. "What exactly is with this circle, then?"

Too bad he'd directed the question to Nico rather than Greta, who answered, "Well, the epicenter is about 400 miles off the coast of Miami."

"Gallagher…" he growled. Not a good start to this conversation.

Before Greta could say anything, Nico plowed ahead. "It seems the majority of the fallout is happening stateside. If there is a threat out there, not to mention an ongoing threat as Greta has suggested, we'd be stupid to ignore it."

"An unknown threat in international waters." Marron tapped a pencil against the map. "No. I'll never get the DoD to sign off on the kind of team you're asking for. They might send in the navy to check it out—"

"No!" Greta might have flung herself across the desk if Nico hadn't been in her way. His arm caught her around the middle, and he swept her behind him, his skin tingling from the intensity of the contact. Her stress and fear wouldn't sell Marron on this mission.

But Nico could do it. He could prove to her that his skill was useful both in the field and to her personally. Maybe then she'd see him as a real partner, potentially beyond the walls of TRAIT, and start to let him in a little. Stop pushing away every time they got closer. "Since we aren't exactly sure what it is we're dealing with, the navy might be overkill."

"Understatement of the year, Tancredi."

At least Marron's attention was back on him rather than on Greta. "But it would be something two agents could check out in a quiet manner. Much cheaper than a full team, and it'll give me some of that field experience I need to really become the kind of agent you hired me to be."

Marron rubbed his jaw and the shadow of stubble that made Nico wonder if the guy had even gone home last night. "The trip would need to be very inexpensive and very quiet if I'm pulling from what little discretionary funding we have." He flipped through the papers while Greta fidgeted at Nico's back. Finally Marron shoved the stack of printouts away. He probably couldn't understand her methods any better than Nico did. "Gallagher, how close to home do you think this hits?"

"Sir?" She moved next to Nico. Her fingers brushed his periodically, as if she wanted him to hold her hand. Under different circumstances, he would have happily obliged, but not here, not now, not if it would undermine the very mission she so badly needed. Then he recognized the intermittent touching for what it was—she was shaking.

"The threat. Nico said it's moving inland. Do you think it comes from our own people or someone else?"

Why would he ask that? Nico was pretty sure Greta hadn't mentioned the conspiracy theory to anyone else, and he knew he hadn't, but if their boss was already thinking it, too, it was seriously bad news. Nico examined Marron's countenance again. Dark circles were forming under his eyes, and in addition to the stubble, his normally impeccable clothes were wrinkled. Even his tie was loosened. Whatever had him in this state couldn't be good for the agency.

Greta shook her head. "I don't know. But there isn't a doubt in my mind that it's bad."

"How bad?"

"Do you remember Cal's mission at the science-fiction convention, where the arms dealer tried to demo the new nerve gas he was selling?"

"Yeah. Takamaki. Thankfully no one died, but there are still people suffering the effects of what gas *did* get out."

"Well, I'm pretty sure this is worse than Takamaki bad."

Marron blew out a breath as if he was exhaling the last bit of energy left in his body. "Greta, finish your research. Nico, make the plan and the travel arrangements. I'll email you with a max budget—try like hell to stay under it. Hit up Cal for some fake IDs for the flight and hotel. I do not want your mission traced back to this office under any circumstances. Is that understood?"

Nico nodded, snatching up Greta's things and ushering her toward the door, his hand on the small of her back. The sooner they were out of here the less likely Marron would be to change his mind. "Crystal clear, sir." He didn't breathe again until the door clicked shut, separating them from their boss.

"That was more difficult than expected." Greta took her papers, then spun toward the stairs that led to their dungeon office.

"You're welcome," Nico muttered under his breath. Clearly, he was seeing things that weren't there with her. There would be no celebratory kiss after getting the mission approved. He might as well go talk to Cal right away. Then a sound stopped him in his tracks.

"And thank you for your help. I don't think he would have said yes to me. I really couldn't ask for a better partner."

By the time Nico came to his senses and spun back

around, Greta was gone. But she'd noticed. With a smile on his face and a spring in his step, Nico did his best not to dance through the hallways. He was going to make this the most flawless mission ever.

And get the girl…of course.

Chapter Seven

Fumbling toward Ecstasy

Greta tugged at the strap of her sundress. She was on a mission, not vacation. It felt wrong to be wearing something so…airy.

Then again, Nico's arm around her waist felt equally wrong. Yet somehow also right. She wanted to lean into him and drink up the contact. The warmth, the security…the absolute wrongness of feeling this for her partner.

And that was the worst part—she didn't know how to feel about his closeness or the distraction it presented. "Do we have to walk like this?"

"We're supposed to be married and looking to move down here, so yes, it's a good idea for us to look young and in love." He cast her a sidelong glance as they neared the building. "I suppose we could hold hands instead, but this seemed more married, less dating."

Thinking back to the couples she was familiar with, Nico probably knew what he was talking about, but this was a first for her. Would the other people recognize that, though? Would they see the way her body leaned toward his, wanting more? Or was that what the honeymoon stage looked like? Trevor and Marissa weren't the best source material for that answer. She'd have to trust her partner. "This is fine."

The truth was it was better than fine. His hand fit perfectly against the curve of her waist, and the weight of his arm felt like it was meant to protect her. The sensation was so foreign she simply didn't know how to deal with it. Nor did she know if it was real.

Correction, she knew it was real for her; she didn't know if it was real for him. Nothing had happened between them since the kiss in their office, but was that because she'd made backing off very clear or because he wasn't interested? With him holding her like this, he felt interested, and she couldn't deny her body's reaction to him.

Too bad Nico's talent lay in getting people to believe things. He'd never managed it when talking to her, but what about this and the way she felt when she kissed him? Was she falling prey to one of his ploys, or was there something more between them? And if there was something now, what did that mean for later when they had to share a hotel room to keep up their ruse—and save TRAIT money?

Just the thought of sharing that space overnight—much less sharing a king-size bed—set her skin tingling. How was she supposed to ignore her desires there? How was she supposed to ignore him? What if he slept in the nude? They hadn't discussed it, and if he was naked next to her…

"What's got your mind spinning so fast, Trouble?"

Greta shook off her musings as much as she could manage. Granted, she was still imagining him naked in bed, but there wasn't much to be done about that at the moment. Fortunately, there had been one thing on her worry list that she could talk about without sounding stupid. "I'm just hoping

Mr. Perfect is okay while I'm gone."

"Yeah. About that. Does Mr. Perfect have a name?" Nico's voice was oddly tight when he asked.

"Yes. It's Mr. Perfect. Why else would I call him that?"

Nico drew to a stop in front of the school, his muscles tense around her. "Okay, then who the hell is he?"

Greta blinked, trying to separate the conversation from the way his muscles flexing against her body felt. Why did he care? "He's my cat. You must have seen him at least once."

The tension fled his body, yet he drew her a little closer. "You named your cat Mr. Perfect?"

"That was his name when I adopted him." He was a cat. He didn't care what his name was, only that someone took care of him and paid him a bit of attention on the schedule of his choosing. In many ways, he was perfect.

"Of course it was." Laughing, he pulled open the door and waved her through. "Ladies first."

His touch fell away as she walked inside, and she missed the contact immediately. Then it was back, his hand cupping her side, lending her a strength that was likely nothing more than the illusion of some bond between them. Unless it *was* more, unless it was real, which didn't make sense. And that was completely driving her insane.

They stood at a counter, and a woman with a slightly graying bun glanced up from her computer. "Can I help you?"

Greta was so lost in her thoughts about Nico and the heat simmering between them, she completely forgot all the things she'd practiced with Marissa the past couple days. The carefully constructed alter-ego went out the window, and the secretary got a full dose of Greta. "That is your job, isn't it?"

As soon as the words were out of her mouth, she knew they were wrong, but it was too late to take them back.

Nico stepped in, laughing, the sound soothing over Greta's nerves. "Not everyone enjoys your sarcastic humor as much as I do." After squeezing Greta tighter—letting her know through the gesture that everything would be okay— he nodded toward the secretary. Too comfortable, far too comfortable if this was all an act. The urge to get away from him before she made another inappropriate advance flared inside as he said, "We have an appointment with Principal Deville."

"Oh, you're the couple who is looking to move to the area. He mentioned you'd be coming in. Right this way." The secretary led them down a short hallway and into an office.

Greta chose to focus on concrete data rather than the strange things she felt around her partner. Hopefully it would prove enough of a distraction from his closeness to get through this meeting.

She had obviously worked for Marron too long. She'd grown accustomed to his love of gray and the starkness of his desk. The principal's office was something else entirely. The desk was a wooden monstrosity that looked as if children had carved the legs. The designs there made little sense to her mind. And the rest of the office followed in the same vein. Drawings and paintings, riotous with color, adorned the wall in bright green frames.

And the man behind the desk didn't seem to fit at all. He wore a jacket and subdued tie—conservative. He was bald and kept his thick mustache neatly trimmed, using wax to curl up the ends—evil. Then he smiled and his eyes sparkled with an inner light—the kind she'd only ever seen in children— playful. While she still didn't understand how he could possibly work in this environment, at least it suited him—his office was as confusing as the picture he himself presented.

Jacob Deville stuck out his hand. "Mr. and Mrs. Johnson, it's a pleasure to meet you."

Alias. My alias is Grace Johnson. Nico is my husband, Neil. Nico shook the man's hand without hesitation. "The pleasure is ours. Your school is lovely."

Greta merely nodded a greeting as Deville shook her hand, as it was obvious with how she'd handled the secretary that she shouldn't do the talking here unless forced. Nico was managing it all, incredibly well in fact. Or at the very least, he didn't seem to be fighting the urge to shake out of his skin at every touch. "It seems a very"—she glanced around the office, desperate for something appropriate to say—"colorful place."

The principal grinned, showing a double row of perfect teeth. No, not quite perfect, one incisor crossed slightly over the other. Once she saw it, she couldn't look away until he closed his mouth. "We like to keep the children's brains active, and we've found that color has a strong effect on their behavior. You'll notice that our walls are painted to reflect this. The library and many classrooms are green because it promotes concentration, whereas the counselor and nurse's offices are blue to be soothing…"

Nico nodded and kept the principal talking by saying all the right things in all the right places. She liked this side of her partner. It was sexy how he could slip into the persona he'd made and roll with everything—including her outburst at the secretary's desk. Most other agents would have done anything they could to get her out of the room after that, but Nico didn't, he kept her even closer.

It was as if he knew her talents were just as valuable, if not more so, than his. While he kept the principal busy, Greta allowed herself to look around for anything here that might hint at foul play where the missing students were concerned. There was nothing. Not a picture out of place, not a file sticking out. How on earth were they supposed to find out anything from the school? This was a waste of time.

She was ready to tell Nico precisely that when he responded to something the principal had just said about school security. "I noticed the cameras and secondary door locks when we came into the building. I'm sure the school itself is safe. I'm somewhat more concerned about walking and bussing routes—when the kids aren't under as much supervision."

The strange tone Nico pushed into his voice when using his gift was there, but the principal didn't respond. For a long minute, the three of them sat there, not a word said among them, and Greta fought the urge to squirm. As much as she liked watching Nico take the lead, there were bad things going on. They needed to get back on the case. This stop had been Nico's idea, and it had been a total waste of...

"I'm guessing you read about the two children who went missing. It was eighteen months ago, but it feels like just yesterday." Principal Deville sighed—the long pause seemed to have been a moment to collect himself rather than any sort of evasion. "Good kids—both of them. They'd walked home together every day, all year, rain or shine. On nice days they liked to walk near the beach. Other children were often with them. That particular day was beautiful—bright and sunny with a perfect blue sky. The other kids stopped to play in the sand, but they said Michelle and Patrick were rushing home so they could help their mother bake a cake. Two blocks. That's all they had left to walk, but they never made it home."

He scrubbed a hand over suddenly weary eyes and blew out a breath. "Teachers and parents have been monitoring walking paths as well as bus stops ever since. Believe me when I say this tragedy hit us all."

And the danger most definitely hadn't come from here. Even with how difficult it was for Greta to read most people, Principal Deville was more like a child in many ways than an adult, and his emotions were completely transparent. He felt personally responsible for whatever had happened to those two kids.

And Nico had narrowed down their search area to two blocks.

Perhaps he wasn't wasting their time after all. And maybe, just maybe, his ability had more uses than getting Marron to agree to missions. He'd gotten them into the school and obtained information she would have likely failed to get via interrogation. A clandestine mission like this required a subtlety she was ill-suited for but was custom-made for the likes of Nico Tancredi.

It also didn't hurt that she found him incredibly attractive when he took charge. Maybe they'd have to have a repeat of that kissing experiment from a few days ago.

No. They really shouldn't do that.

Should they?

Without thinking about it, Greta stuck her pinky between her teeth.

After the school, they went in search of the marine biologists who had been quoted in the article on the dolphins. They'd been less than helpful, only confirming what Greta had said about how normally a single dolphin might lose a fight with sharks, but that it was incredibly odd for two of them to wash ashore, largely uneaten. One of them simply shrugged off further inquiry with "But what else could have done that sort of damage?"

What indeed?

Other than that, the scientists hadn't remembered many details of the incident.

Many of the other articles Greta had found probably wouldn't amount to much of anything, so Nico decided to focus on the weirdest, and therefore most likely, of the bunch. "Last stop."

"Good." Greta rubbed at her arms. "I feel like we're running out of time somehow."

She was on edge. Some damage control was necessary before she ended up biting off a finger. "Time? We could talk about time. How about we trade quotes from *Somewhere in Time*?"

She rolled her eyes. "No. And this is hardly time for joking."

"Did you say it's time for jokes? *Time Bandits* was pretty funny."

Her lips twitched. "Stop it. We're trying to keep people from being killed."

"You're totally right. *A Time to Kill* was no joking matter."

"Stop!"

"Hammer time? Wait. That's not a movie."

Greta snorted a tiny laugh, but her dimple was out. Success!

Granted the dimple disappeared in a few brief seconds, but he knew better than to expect more than that. "Feeling better?"

"Yes. Thank you." She drummed her fingers on the armrest, a motion much calmer than most of her tics. "I just feel like we need to finish this and get on the ocean."

"Well, we can't take off until tomorrow, and this is our last stop. We'll buzz by the marina and confirm the boat reservation for morning." He threw the car into park and killed the engine.

Greta nodded rapidly as she stepped onto the concrete. "Okay. That's reasonable enough."

They walked into the beachside police department, and he flashed fake press credentials at the desk. The officer there jerked his head toward the rear left corner of the station. "Go on back. The chief's been waiting for you."

The chief of police met them at the door. She was five

ten, maybe five eleven—it was hard for Nico to tell for sure because the boots she wore had heels that put her taller than him—and her hair was styled in a short, no-nonsense cut. It was as if she knew a lot of people would have a tough time respecting a woman in her position and wanted to make it perfectly clear she could play with the boys—including the big ones. "Fitzgerald and Monroe, right?"

Nico nodded as he took a seat. "That's right. We're doing a piece on the bath salts craze for the *Chicago Register*, and when my partner saw there'd been a second overdose that involved cannibalism, we knew we wanted to talk to you personally."

The role of interrogating reporter was one Greta could pull off without too much self-control, so Nico had encouraged her to take part in the conversation. Her desire to be done with this clearly made her willing to play along. "Was there anything strange? Something that might differentiate your 2014 case from the one in 2012? Different levels of the drugs in the man's system, perhaps?"

The chief just shook her head. "Like I tried to explain on the phone, there's not a lot I can tell you."

"Because the investigation is still open? Surely with the perpetrator dead, you can hardly be looking at charging him with a crime."

"No, Miss Monroe. I can't help you because we didn't get to keep the body."

Greta's fingers began clenching and unclenching on the arm of her chair. She was more tense than Nico had realized, and this new bit of information seemed like it might push her over the edge. "What do you mean, you didn't keep the body?" he asked.

After shrugging as if this sort of thing happened every day, the chief said, "*Mr. Smith's*"—she paused to let the likely fake identity sink in—"next of kin claimed his corpse before we could even perform a rudimentary autopsy. Signed an affidavit saying they had no intention of pressing charges against the officers who shot him and that they just wanted to give their cousin a proper burial."

"And you gave it to them?" Greta almost jumped out of her chair.

The chief fixed a heavy gaze on the two of them and said, very calmly, "Two men in suits, with the most perfect set of papers I've ever seen in all my years on the force, came into this room and claimed the body of their cousin. As you already stated, it wasn't as if we could charge the corpse with a crime. And the men were incredibly insistent."

Nico's mouth went dry. He'd seen the look she was giving them. He had a feeling she'd tell them everything without much persuasion, but he pushed a bit of his gift into his voice anyway. "The papers. Too good to be true?"

"You could say that."

"Very official looking? Possibly fresh from a government office?"

"You could say that, too. In fact, the papers included Mr. Smith's recent discharge orders from the navy—which conveniently included allegations of drug use. There wasn't a single piece left out of the puzzle."

"That's…interesting."

"Isn't it, Mr. Fitzgerald?" The chief tapped a file on her desk. "It's also very interesting that, after the initial news story, everything about the case was buried…except our report. And I'm still less than pleased about all of it. So, I'm going to be really generous here and offer you a copy of our entire file—what there is—without you needing to ask for it. But, sadly, there's nothing more I can tell you that isn't in these papers." She held out the file, but paused when Nico went to take it. "Keep my name out of things, Mr. Fitzgerald. I don't know who those men really were, but I'm uninterested in a return visit from them."

Greta was already out of her chair and on her way to the door when Nico stood. "Understood, Chief, and thank you."

After a cursory glance at the file, two things were very clear: first, someone high up in the government wanted this killing covered up on all fronts; and two, none of the locals had discovered the link between the seemingly unconnected troubles he and Greta were investigating. Which left them in almost the same place they'd started—a whole lot of questions and not much in the way of answers.

Nico rubbed at his forehead with one hand while he steered the car with the other. Greta, on the other hand, had her laptop balanced on her thighs, taking notes as she read through the file on "Mr. Smith." They'd been running all day, how could she keep going full-steam like this? And damn it, he'd like five minutes alone with her where they weren't all-mission-all-the-time. "It's getting late. Maybe it's time to get some dinner and check into the hotel so we can hit the trail hard again tomorrow."

Greta blinked as if she hadn't noticed the sun setting. "It *is* getting late. Can we just call to confirm the boat for morning?"

"Best idea I've heard all day." He pulled his phone from his pocket and hit the marina's number. As soon as the guy on the other end went through his hello spiel, Nico said, "Hi, this is Neil Johnson. My wife Grace and I just wanted to confirm our boat rental for tomorrow."

"Oh. Didn't you get our text, Mr. Johnson?"

If Nico hadn't been driving, he would have glared at the phone. "What text is that?"

"Two of our boats had to go for emergency maintenance. As you and your wife were the last reservations, you were the first we had to cancel. Obviously, we will do everything we can to rectify this…"

"Can you book us another boat for tomorrow?" Nico didn't have to look to know that Greta was tensing up again—probably chewing on her finger. Damn it.

"Unless we have a pair of cancellations or the repairs are done a lot faster than anticipated, no. We can change your reservation to the next day—we still have a couple openings. Or we can refund your deposit."

Fuck. "Keep it for now. We want a boat tomorrow morning if at all possible. We'll be at the marina early, looking for other options, though."

"I understand, sir. And if there's anything else I can do to accommodate you, don't hesitate to ask."

Nico scowled as he stabbed the button to end the call. "Yeah, you can find us another boat, jackass."

"We don't have a boat." Greta said it so quietly, he almost didn't hear her.

"No, but we'll get one."

"I guess that means the marina before the hotel. We need transportation."

Of course they did, and by her voice she meant they needed it now, which wasn't happening. "We'll have better luck in the morning. A lot of charter offices are likely closed for the night."

"But if we don't have one tonight, we can't leave in the morning." Her voice had the no-nonsense tone he'd come to associate with her recognizing when he was trying to sway her way of thinking.

Damn it. He'd done it without realizing, but he didn't want her to get pissed because she assumed he was trying to manipulate her. "Okay. We'll *try*, but you may have to accept that we probably won't find anything tonight."

"I don't have to accept anything."

Yet. She didn't have to accept anything yet. But if the traffic was any indication, she would soon. Cars lined the road in all lanes going both directions. Bumper to bumper with exhaust fumes making the air waver more than the heat did. At least there weren't any accidents—Nico had the police scanner on, mainly to avoid unnecessary traffic delays. Unfortunately it appeared this was just normal evening traffic in Miami. "It might not be a bad idea to make some phone calls, narrow down our options to the ones that are possible."

After Greta left a third irate message, he was starting to regret the suggestion. She frowned and clutched the phone tighter. "What good is it for me to leave a message when you won't be open again until morning? I need a boat *in the morning*." She stabbed at the phone, then poked a finger at Nico. "You need to drive faster."

"Sure thing. I'll just pull the lever that turns our rental car into a tank and barrel right over all these civilians."

"Sarcasm."

She said it as a statement, but in case it was meant as a question, Nico responded, "Yes, Trouble. Even if I had the technology, I wouldn't use it here."

"I don't like it."

"What?"

"The delay." The way she fidgeted spoke to much more than an uncomfortable passenger seat.

Maybe they should have split up today. He could have hit all the known sites and she could have confirmed their ride for tomorrow—and then gone on the hunt for a new one when things turned into a clusterfuck. *Shoulda, woulda, coulda. Didn't. That's the only part that matters now.* "Look, we'll do what we can. I promise, one way or another, we'll get out there and figure out what the hell is going on."

"Since when do you make promises you can't keep?"

"Since never." And he planned on keeping this one. Granted, he didn't see how there would be any major hiccups in the way, only some delays if they couldn't get a boat for the morning, but he'd deal with that if and when it happened.

As soon as they dumped the car at their hotel, they made their way to the docks, only to find that Nico had been right. All the offices were dark and locked up tight. They managed to find one fishing boat captain still aboard his ship, but he laughed them off. "It's winter. People come down here from the great frozen north to enjoy the sun and the water. I'm booked up solid this week—a lot of us are. What did you expect? To just walk onto a boat and have it ready to go?"

As soon as Greta tensed next to him, Nico smiled and said, "More like we were hoping someone would suddenly end up double-booked if there was enough incentive."

The captain's bushy mustache twitched as if he were sniffing the air for money. "Some might, but you're better off looking for pleasure sailings than fishing charters. We get booked up by bachelor parties and the like. The other ships have no-shows more often than we do. They might be willing to piss off a couple tourists if the money is right."

Nico nodded. It might not be a reservation, but it was good information to have. He pressed a twenty into the guy's palm as he shook his hand. "Thanks."

The captain eyeballed the cash but didn't say a word as he pocketed it. Nico ushered a flustered Greta off the boat.

"Why does this seem like you're giving up? We need a boat."

"And we'll get a boat. Just not tonight. Tonight we're going to get food and some rest instead." And somehow, Nico was going to get Greta to relax and let her guard down a little. There was a narrow window of opportunity here between starting the mission by getting on the plane this morning and starting in earnest by getting on a boat tomorrow. No matter what else happened tonight, he was going to make the most of what little time he had.

The hotel door would have slammed had it not been weighted to prevent such things from happening. Greta swung it for all she was worth, but it simply slowed as it neared the latch, then clicked shut. She frowned at the thing, believing in her heart that if it would have only slammed, things wouldn't be so messed up.

Her head knew better.

Today had been a total waste of time—regardless of what they'd learned at the school and the police station. She'd told Nico the problem was in the Atlantic, but he'd reminded her that Marron would have been pissed about them spending money if there was clear evidence the problems were something normal…and worse, unconnected.

But she couldn't quite wrap her mind around the idea of spending an entire day in Florida and getting nothing for their trouble. The thought made the muscle in her shoulder twitch, and as soon as that started, she knew she was in trouble. Soon enough, her fingernail found its way to her teeth, just to keep her from screaming.

"Hey, stop it." Nico tugged her hand from her mouth, massaging her palm with his thumbs. They stood like that for a long minute, him applying pressure to the oddly sensitive flesh of her hands. Touching. Too much touching if they were just going to be partners. But she didn't want it to stop, at least not until he said, "You're stressed out. Do you have one of your tops in your purse or overnight bag?"

She didn't like that he recognized her need to have something to fidget with. And she really didn't like that he knew she'd need one more than she had. "No."

"Good thing I'm looking out for you then." He pulled a little plastic top from his pocket. "I picked this up at the gas station on our way here. Just in case."

There were a pair of dolphins chasing each other across the surface—the irony of that wasn't lost on her, but then again neither was the rush of comfort that simply holding it brought. The thing had probably come from a machine and cost less than a dollar, but it meant a lot more than that to her. She clutched it in her fist, letting the edges of the plastic bite into her skin for a second before she collapsed in the chair by the desk and set the little toy spinning. Around and around it went, and she watched as the design on the inside spiraled into a blur and worked its magic, mesmerizing her and easing the tension from her shoulders.

Or perhaps that was more the result of Nico's fingers kneading at her muscles. She'd been so lost in the solace of the spinning top that she hadn't noticed him for a second. Now he was the only thing holding her attention—the roughness of the calluses on his fingertips, the strength in his hands, and the gentleness, too. It felt real. Too real. Too perfect. "What are you doing?"

"Trying to help you relax." His thumbs pressed into the hollows between her shoulder blades. "Unless it's bothering you. I mean, I can stop if it is."

The massage felt good, soothing, and she liked having his hands on her. Perhaps more than she should, but he didn't need to know that. After all her missteps earlier, she needed to be objective now. He wasn't flirting; he couldn't be. He was just being a good partner—ensuring she was at her best for the mission. She wasn't about to make him uncomfortable by admitting more than she should. She would just enjoy the feel of his skin on hers for as long as he let her. She could do that without making a fool of herself—again. "No. You don't need to stop."

The top skittered over the desktop and stalled by her fingers, flopping onto its side as if all the stress had been erased. Perhaps her worries over their delays had been, but Nico's closeness was bringing its own sort of tension—regardless of how tightly she was keeping her lips sealed and promising herself she'd behave. She wanted more, wanted all of him.

What she *needed* was a distraction. Preferably something that would help with the mission and the rest of her work at TRAIT.

As seemed to be becoming a theme with them, Nico provided—only not in the way she'd hoped. "I have to ask—you've kissed me twice. Was that an experiment and it's over and done now, or are more sneak-attack make-out sessions in our future?"

Every ounce of stress he'd massaged from her shoulders promptly rushed right back in. He'd asked so nonchalantly—as if the answer didn't matter to him—that she had no idea how to respond. So she took the only logical option and threw the question back at him. "Which would you prefer?"

His hands paused in their ministrations, and the next thing Greta knew, he'd spun the chair around until she faced him. With the way he leaned over, bracketing her into the chair with his arms, she was enveloped by him. She dove into the darkness of his eyes as she inhaled the scent of wind and sea from his skin. She wanted to touch him, touch herself, touch anything to do with how he made her feel. Instead, she just gripped the arms of the chair.

"I would *prefer* we not dance around this until we're old and gray. I would *prefer* not to have to risk my job to get past whatever we're doing, but the thing I'd most *prefer* would be if you'd just shut up and kiss me already." When Greta didn't move beyond her gaze shifting to his lips, Nico amended, "Or I can just do what I should have done all along."

The distance between them disappeared, and his lips were on hers, firm but soft and yielding. Neither of them were drunk. Neither of them were pushing away. And when Nico traced the seam of her mouth with his tongue, Greta's entire body lit on fire, and neither of them held back.

Nico might not have been able to work his magic on her when he spoke, but with this new use of his lips and tongue, she was helpless to resist him. Every shred of her logic and inhibitions vanished as he nipped her lower lip and sucked on it. All sensation flowed from that bit of flesh. Her mouth felt alive, and her kisses turned desperate, hungrier. She'd wanted all of him, and now it seemed he was more than willing to give it to her.

She didn't realize her fingers were working at the buttons of his shirt, though, until Nico slowly pulled away from the kiss. "Greta?"

"Shut up, take your clothes off, and have sex with me already." That was what she wanted—him, inside her, every inch of them touching.

"No."

"No?" Had she somehow misjudged that kiss? Did she read all of this wrong? Again?

"No, I won't do that. I will, however, keep talking to you, because I fucking like talking to you. And I'll take *your* clothes off because I want to touch you more than I want to breathe half the time."

Oh. *Yes, please.* That sounded like heaven. Or the tortures of hell… "And the sex?"

"Trouble, if we're getting naked and making out, we're having sex. That's a given."

"Good. I like sex." Even though she hadn't had it in a very long time. She felt silly saying it the way she had, but Nico didn't seem to mind at all. He only gave her that adorably crooked smile and held out his hands.

Those magical hands. She let her fingers drift over the roughness of them, and he let out a little shudder at the contact. She was doing something wrong again… But when she moved to pull back, he gripped her fingers. "Don't. I want you to touch me, too. We have all night to learn each other."

Biting her swollen lip, Greta nodded. Sooner or later, she had to accept the fact that Nico understood her—or at the very least that he wanted to. He clearly wasn't going to run scared. He wasn't going to make fun of her. No, he was going to do what he always did and try to make this as perfect as he could.

One cream, three sugars, just the way you like it.

Blowing out a slow breath, she closed her eyes and let her fingertips skate over his hands again. When she looked at him once more, she curled her fingers in his and let him pull her to her feet. This close, his breath ruffled the hair against her cheek and sent a shiver down her spine. If doing just this with him was already so intense, how was she going to handle more?

When he eased the strap of her sundress off her shoulder and his lips followed in its wake, she realized the only path to surviving with her mind intact was just to let go and give in to the sensations. His mouth blazed a trail of heat so intense she arched into it, and her knees threatened to stop holding her up. Already, her body was screaming for more. She was on fire with need, but he didn't stop the slow, delicious torture.

The dress fell into a puddle around her feet, and those amazing hands swept over her. Her abdomen, then her thighs, down to her ankles, and then back up to cup her ass as he kissed and nipped at the skin just above her panties.

She was glad he held her because it was all she could do to breathe and cling to his shoulders as he pressed his mouth against the silken fabric, kissing her there, the heat of his mouth joining with the wet heat that filled her.

This wasn't sex, at least not any sex like she'd ever known. She wasn't even naked yet, and already her body was awash in Nico. He was all she could feel, all she could think about.

Then he hooked his fingers under the fabric of her panties and inched them down her legs. No kisses now, but she could feel the intensity of his gaze as shivers raced through her at his touch.

Nico made a noise in the back of his throat as he kissed her hip. It sounded like a growl, and Greta melted. Fortunately, as her knees finally gave up any pretense of strength, he caught her, his grip firm on her ass once more. When he looked up, there was a heat in his eyes she'd never seen before. "Bed. Now."

His voice held a deepness that was new, almost gravelly. It wasn't that he was trying to use his gift on her. This was different. Something special…just for her. For the first time in her life, Greta finally understood what women meant when they said a man made them melt.

She was on the bed before she had time to think about the fact that she was taking orders from him. Nothing mattered except this moment. Not their jobs. Not the mission. For one blissful pocket of time—the world narrowed to her and Nico.

Once she was on her back, he spread her thighs, laying her bare before him. His rough palms scraped against the smoothness of her legs as he moved, and even that sensation was fraught with sexual tension, building her need to the point that she no longer cared about control. She no longer cared about anything but having him inside her. By the time his tongue found her folds, Greta was already gripping the sheets. It had been too long.

No. It was the perfect amount of time for me to find him.

Not even that thought was enough to scare her away. This was right. No, this was perfect.

Her eyes rolled back as he found her center and pressed one, then two fingers into her depths. It was too much. But it wasn't enough. She let go and gave herself up to him completely. For the first time in her life, nothing was holding her down, holding her back. Free. She felt totally free to do or say whatever her mind and body demanded, so she did. "More. I need more."

Nico obliged, sucking on her clit until the building orgasm arched her back off the bed. There was no more thought. There was only Nico.

And no matter how long it had taken them to find each other, he had most definitely been worth the wait.

Chapter Eight

One Wild Night

She tasted like heaven. Nico could have happily stayed between Greta's thighs like this all night long, but she clearly wanted more—and so did he. The minute she arched off the mattress, he knew he better pull back a little or they'd be done far too soon for his taste. Her muscles contracted, squeezing his fingers as she came.

Reluctantly, he moved from her clit to press kisses to her thighs.

"Done already?" her voice slurred with that exquisite combination of desire and release.

"Not by a long shot." He crawled up her body, tracing patterns on her skin with his tongue. "I just want to make sure I don't wear you out too fast." Once he settled in next to her, he let his fingers find her clit again and rubbed it in gentle, lazy circles. Not enough to make her come again. Just enough pressure so there wasn't a chance in hell she'd forget what they were doing.

For a while, they lay there, just like that, making out and touching each other all over. Until Greta gripped Nico's erection.

The sudden need to not only be with her, but to be *in* her, coursed through him. "You want that?"

"More than anything."

That single phrase was almost enough to push him over the edge. He took a few seconds to regain control, then promptly rolled Greta onto her back, pinning her wrists to the mattress. "It's probably a good thing Marissa packed for us then."

Greta squirmed beneath him, rubbing her wetness along the length of his engorged cock until he groaned. "Why is that?"

"She decided we needed condoms." He leaned down and sucked her nipple into his mouth. Reluctantly he let go. "Be right back."

He raced to the bathroom and returned in record time. It wasn't that he was afraid Greta would change her mind so much as he was afraid she'd start overthinking things again. It was what Marissa had told him she was doing with the whole kissing and then backing off thing. If he wanted Greta, he needed to take charge and stop with all the gentle prodding and hints.

Even with only being gone a few seconds, she was already propped on her elbows when he came back into the room, rolling the condom onto his length. Her eyes flashed to his dick for a second, but then she looked him right in the eyes. "Are you sure this is a good idea?"

"I'm sure it's the best idea I've ever had. And I'm absolutely positive it's the only idea I'm going to have right now. Everything else can wait. We can't." He slid his hand up her leg, waiting for her to argue, waiting for her to disappear on him. Praying she wouldn't.

Instead, she bit her full lower lip and nodded. "You're right."

He didn't give her time to change her mind. Nico kissed his way up her thighs again, parting them once more to lave her with his tongue. Wet and ready, waiting just for him. The head of his cock pressed against her slit, and she spread her legs wider, opening herself to him. Her eyes rolled back as he slid home. She was so tight, her muscles gripping him as he moved in and out, thrusting slowly with his full length until Greta was fisting the sheets. She felt so good around him, he hated to stop, but the whole sheet thing would never do.

One at a time, he peeled her hands off the fabric. "I want you touching me—holding on to *me*—when you come. This isn't about anything but us."

She grabbed his biceps, her nails digging in as he started pumping faster. "Harder. As hard as you can."

That was one demand he had no qualms about giving in to. He pounded into her, thrusting with every ounce of strength he had. The headboard was attached to the hotel wall, but the bed itself rocked, banging against the wall in rhythm with the meeting of their bodies. Greta's eyelids fluttered, and her fingers clawed down his arms, nails digging in, seconds before her inner muscles contracted as she came.

He kept thrusting, faster and faster as she rode out the waves of her orgasm. He'd never seen her more beautiful than she was right now, her head thrown back with abandon, cheeks flushed with desire, breasts jutting toward the ceiling. And watching her as she came tipped him right over the edge. His orgasm followed on the heels of hers, stealing his breath and making his body go rigid.

When he was spent, his arms started shaking from holding the position for so long. He collapsed on top of her and rolled them both until they were on their sides, joined in a tangle of limbs and lovemaking. It had been more perfect than he'd ever imagined—and he'd imagined this more times than he wanted to count.

Nico could hardly breathe, much less talk, but Greta murmured, "You were so right—we already waited too long for that."

G reta's eyes rolled into her head as she sank into Nico's embrace. For a brief moment, she felt utterly at peace with the world. If this was what she'd been missing by not having a partner all this time, she wanted to kick herself. Better yet, she'd have Marissa kick her—that would be much more effective.

Of course, beyond sex, she'd also been missing the assistance of a different mode of operations. Nico had done a stellar job of getting them in places and obtaining information. She'd said it was useless, but that had just been her frustration talking. To really get solid data to take back to Marron, they needed all the evidence they could get their hands on—and she sucked at that.

Sure, Greta was great with the internet and interpreting random bits of data. Nico, on the other hand, was amazing with people. Without him, she'd have still been back in Naperville trying to figure out why her data points didn't fit a pattern. He'd wanted to learn how she did her work. Perhaps it would be a good idea for her to learn more about his gift as well.

"Nico?"

"Hmmm?" His thumbs moved up her spine and started rubbing at her neck.

She wanted to lean into his touch and say all sorts of things that would cause them all sorts of awkwardness on the job. Then again, weren't they past that particular point of no return? But she'd had a plan before his hands had started working their magic. *Focus on learning about him…while he turns your entire body to Jell-O.* She murmured, "Tell me how it works? Your…thing."

"My *thing*?" His voice had a lilt to it that wasn't normally present, as if he were holding back the urge to laugh.

Greta tried not to let the feeling get to her. She had responded in a similar fashion when other people tried to understand her own work. "Not your penis. I know how that works, and yours works very well. I meant the way you manipulate people."

Nico's fingers tightened on her shoulders for a second, and she winced, then his hands were gone. "Let's get something straight. I don't manipulate people."

The temperature in the room seemed to have dropped more than a couple degrees in the last few seconds, and Greta shivered as she turned. "What would you call it then?"

"I talk to them in a way that opens them up to possibilities. That helps them *want* to talk to me or believe me."

She thought back to the moment he'd called her a psychic and couldn't see how this conversation was so very different. "And how exactly is that not manipulation?"

She hadn't put any judgment into her tone. In fact, she'd gone out of her way to make her voice as neutral as possible, but Nico raked his hand through his hair violently as if she'd thrown the worst insult in the world at him. That wasn't what she'd meant—at all—but she didn't know how to take it back.

"To me, manipulating people means lying to get them to do what you want. What I do is use just enough of the truth to nudge people toward a path they aren't opposed to. I can't *make* someone tell me something if they really don't want to; I'm not truth serum. And I can't make them believe out and out lies. I can bend their perception, lead them down a path, but they have to want to follow me. That's it; that's all I do." His muscles were tight, and he was shifting away from her.

She'd touched on a wound that should have been left alone.

Her instinct was to give him space. That would be what she'd want, but she wasn't Nico. Comfort. He needed comfort. She reached toward him, and he flinched as if she'd struck him instead and rolled to sit on the edge of the bed. She drew her hand back slowly. If he wouldn't let her touch him, how was she supposed to fix this? She didn't have the skill he did with words, but she had to try something. "Nico? What did I do?"

"Nothing."

It wasn't me. It wasn't me. It's going to be okay because it wasn't me.

But it wasn't okay for him, only for her. The way he sat on the edge of the bed, hunched over… She'd seen people act like this before. When she was younger—there had been kids in her class that didn't really talk, but they pulled away at the slightest hint of contact.

She'd done it herself, often, but at least she'd had her voice at her disposal, too. Nico was more like her than like them, she just had to get him talking. And if he was like her, the answer to what was bothering him started to become clear. "Then what did someone else do?"

Nico sat there and shook his head, his movements stiff and jerky. "It doesn't matter. It's in the past."

There was no such thing as *in the past*. Greta knew that all too well—both personally and professionally. In her particular line of work for TRAIT, the past very often came back to haunt people. "It does matter. We're partners. If there is something bothering you…"

"It's not something you can fix."

He was probably right, but it didn't matter, not to her. She needed to know, because it was part of him—and that made it important. "But maybe it is something I can understand."

"I doubt it."

She tried not to let the words sting, but his meaning was

clear. *You can barely understand people at all. What makes you think you can understand this?* But he was wrong, because for the first time she *wanted* to understand this, to understand him. "Can you at least let me try? Can you let me be a friend for once?"

Can you let me be more than that?

She crawled across the bed until she knelt behind him. When he didn't shy away, she leaned in and pressed a kiss to the side of his neck, lingering there to inhale the scent of him in case she'd pushed him away harder than she thought. "Please."

A shiver raced through his body, and she had a feeling it wasn't a good one from her kiss. It was a memory. "We talked about my family last week. I told you they never really cared about me one way or another."

"I remember." It had been a key moment for them. One of trust and bonding. It had been important, too.

"I lied."

"What do you mean, you lied?" The lack of accusation in her tone was nice, but he expected nothing less from Greta. Neutrality was the name of her game most of the time, but it didn't mean she *was* neutral, only that she wasn't going to show her cards. It was a trait he both loved and hated about her.

He scrubbed at his face. The hug had been nice, though. The kiss on his neck, too. If he focused on those things, maybe it'd be enough to get him through. He'd never talked to anyone about this. There'd been no need, and there sure as hell had never been any desire. But now…he felt like he had to tell her, at least if he wanted any chance to keep things moving forward between them. "It was mostly true. Like I said, I play with the truth. Ninety-nine-point-nine percent of the time, my family just pretended I didn't exist. The other point one percent was how I realized I didn't need or want them in my life."

Looking back now, it had been such a stupid thing, but wasn't everything when you were a kid? "I figured out my 'gift' at a young age. I could work the system to get picked for the teams I wanted in gym, get my choice in projects for school. I never saw it as a bad thing because I was only nudging people to a decision they were already pretty good with. And I didn't use it a lot, at least I hadn't thought I did."

"And then something happened." Her hands were around him now, her chin resting on his shoulders, the touch gentle, comforting.

He reached up and took her hands, pulling her tighter to him. Not so long ago, she wouldn't have let him do that. She'd have pulled away, and they'd have been done touching. He wasn't about to risk losing her now, not when he knew for sure he wanted to keep her close.

"And then something happened," he echoed. "My family was debating where to go on vacation. I was the youngest—the extra kid. I made an even number, so I never got a vote. That year we were meeting up with some extended family and the choices were Orlando or camping in Redwood National Park. A week of amusement parks versus a week in the middle of nowhere with a bunch of relatives who were all older than me. My sisters were split, and my brother was the deciding vote. He told me he didn't care, so I nudged him toward Orlando."

"That doesn't sound so bad. If he didn't care, why did it matter?"

Remembering hurt. Not a fist to the gut, but a knife—a sharp one. It cut him open, letting the worst parts of his past spill out while he watched. While she watched.

Wasn't that what couples did, though? Hold on to each

other while going through the painful parts of life? At the moment it felt like the only thing holding him together were her arms around him. It gave him the strength to keep talking, to let all of it out.

"Exactly. *He* didn't care. My parents did. Disney was the more expensive option, but the rule had always been that the kids got to choose. When they found out I swayed my brother's vote, they decided it didn't count and made the call themselves. That would have been bad enough, but while we were on the camping trip from hell, my parents made me stand in front of everyone and publicly apologize for, quote— manipulating my brother and trying to make everyone go broke so I could meet a princess—unquote."

To this day, he remembered standing there, being judged by a bunch of people who were supposed to care about him. Being dwarfed by redwoods was nothing compared to how small they'd made him feel. Never again. "I was eleven years old when I learned that there was no one looking out for me except me."

"Oh, Nico…" Greta pressed her mouth to his neck, but something wetter than her kiss fell onto his shoulder this time. "I'll look out for you, too."

He didn't know why, but those six simple words… It was as if she'd let him get the bad stuff out then stitched him up to try to make him whole once more. And maybe with her, whole wasn't such a crazy dream. He was starting to believe that together, they could do anything.

"Thanks, Trouble." He twisted around and wiped a tear from her cheek. That was a first. "Until this moment, I didn't think you knew how to cry. Are these for me?"

Her lips twitched into a pained smile for a second, then fell. "They're for both of us." Somehow, that knowledge made them mean more, and he drew her from behind him and onto his lap. With her arms around him and her head nestled between his chin and chest, she said, "Why is it that some people have relatives like the ones on *Modern Family*, who all have each other's backs, and some have…what we had?"

Was he not the only one who'd held back? She was usually so direct about everything, he'd never even considered the possibility that she wouldn't tell him everything about her past when he'd asked. "Greta?"

She sniffled and shook her head. "I wasn't abused, either. Not in the direct sense. But my family didn't understand me. They never *tried* to. I was shuffled from one school to another in search of a *fix*. They thought I was broken, crazy maybe, and even when doctors and teachers insisted I just looked at the world differently, they couldn't handle it. I was too smart, too weird, too obsessive, too quiet, too…everything. One of the things that sold me on TRAIT was the way Marron described it."

He remembered that moment like it was yesterday, standing in the warehouse with Finn, wondering what the hell he'd gotten himself into. "We are the redheaded stepchildren of the intelligence community?"

"But we are also the best. Yeah. That felt like me at home. In so many ways, I was the best of my family, but because I didn't fit in, I might as well have not existed. At TRAIT, I mean something, I'm important. In my whole life, I never felt as valued as I did the moment I walked into that building." Another tear fell, this one splashing against her leg. She looked down at it like it was a foreign thing. "And I *do* cry. I just learned not to bother a long time ago."

Nico gathered her into his arms and held her tight. They were so right together it hurt. He only hoped she saw it, too, because he didn't want to let this go, ever. "How the hell— in this whole, wide world of suckage—was I lucky enough to find someone as amazing as you?"

"Because you didn't give up. You didn't stop believing

there was someone out there for you. I did, so thank you for finding me. I didn't realize how tired I was of being lost until you did."

There was no more to say after that. She didn't need to know he'd been lost this whole time, too. He'd gone through his life, expecting nothing from anyone. Then he'd found the most unexpected thing of all—someone who fit so perfectly with him, it was like life had pulled them from their families just so they'd be forced to find each other and become one.

Chapter Nine

What the Water Gave Me

"A boat, a boat, my kingdom for a boat," Nico muttered as they approached yet another charter.

Greta knew he was trying to keep her calm and centered, so she played along, even though all she wanted to do was scream…and then commandeer whatever damn boat they found that was still at the dock. "Wait. You have a kingdom? What the hell are we doing working then?"

"Saving the world. Duh. Otherwise the bad guys take over the kingdom. Definitely not in my ten-year plan."

That actually managed to make her laugh. Nico had been doing the impossible and keeping her calm through all of this mess. Every single boat they found had been in the process of loading up, and their budget hadn't allowed for large enough bribes to sway people into giving up an excursion they were already starting. Greta pointed to a white fishing boat that wasn't quite as shiny as the others had been. "What about that one?"

"On the plus side, it doesn't look like there's a crowd."

They made their way toward the *Salty Sea-Dog*, and a man stepped off the deck. He looked like an '80s hair band reject with the facial hair of a *Pirates of the Caribbean* extra. "'Bout time you got here. I almost took your deposit and ran."

That was a good sign. If they played this right, they'd be on the water and on the way to their mystery spot in less than thirty minutes. Greta nudged Nico, knowing very well it'd be best if she kept her mouth shut.

He stepped forward, grinning. "How close to cut-off?"

"Five minutes. Let's load up and head out." The guy spun to get back on board.

Nico's voice stopped him. "Well, how do you feel about killing their five-minute window and letting us rent your boat for the day instead? You get the day off, and assuming you're in line with other boats in the area, we can pay you an extra fifty percent for claiming your watch is running five minutes fast."

The guy snorted, his inner saltiness coming out. "First, no one pilots my boat but me. Second, why the hell would you pay that much?"

"Because we don't want to wait for our reservation tomorrow on *Poseidon's Dynasty*. The sooner we get to our destination, the sooner we can head home."

His gaze roved over them, taking in Greta's bikini and sarong, as well as the bags of gear by her feet. "Which means you aren't looking to go fishing or just for a nice cruise. Pass."

"Let's try this a different way. You can give us a ride for twice your normal fare, or I can make sure my coast guard friends know to keep a really close eye on the *Salty Sea-Dog*. Interested now?" Clearly Nico had decided to forgo any attempt to get the boat without its captain.

And the threat went over about as well as the suggestion that they sail solo. The guy stormed toward Nico and got right in his face, mustache twitching as he said, "Who the hell are you people?"

Rather than flinching, Nico grinned and waved a fistful of cash at the guy. "Just a couple of happy newlyweds who love a good treasure hunt. My wife here heard about a wreck, and we want to check it out—see if there's anything worth salvaging before some big crew gets there and claims the lot of it."

"Plenty of wrecks in the Atlantic. What makes this one so damned special? And I don't do salvage work without a share." He stroked his beard like it was a cat, and Greta had the absurd image of Mr. Perfect perched on the guy's face.

"Because it's not public yet. We weren't supposed to hear about it at all—so the timing is perfect. And we'll cut you in at ten percent."

"Twenty-five."

"Fifteen."

"Twenty."

"Done," Nico said, grinning. He turned and winked at Greta. "Where exactly do we need to go, dear?"

It had been so sexy watching him work, Greta almost forgot to answer. "Oh, twenty-five degrees north, seventy degrees west."

"The triangle? All this to hit the triangle? There's nothing out there but a bunch of water and superstition. What are you, some sort of supernatural nuts?" Nico shrugged, probably thinking of the TV show again, but it was clearly enough of an answer for the man. He pulled a baseball cap out of his back pocket and settled it over his mass of curls. "Fine, I'm Captain Ryan. Get on board, and I'll take you to your spot in the middle of nowhere."

When he grabbed for the cash, Nico drew back, counting out bills and handing him several. "Regular fee now, bonus after. Don't want to risk you leaving us out there."

"Because I dump bodies in the Atlantic regularly." Captain Ryan shook his head, but he didn't stop them from boarding, and in minutes, they were on their way.

Once they were out on the open ocean, Greta rose from her spot inside the cabin, planning to step outside. She hadn't been on the water like this before. She wanted to feel the salty sea breeze on her skin. The seat cushion shifted as she stood though. "Nico?"

He glanced over from the kitchen area, where he'd been grabbing a bottle of water. "What is it?"

She pointed at the seating area. "Why did that move?"

Shrugging, he pulled on the cushion to reveal the storage compartment beneath. "Fairly standard in boats."

That might be true enough, but looking in this one, Greta had a hard time believing it was that simple. She pointed at the gear stowed inside. "Everything is on the ends. Why? It's a completely illogical system."

Nico shrugged. "I'm game for an adventure—you know, besides the one we're already on. And with Captain Spongybeard Crankypants in the wheelhouse, we could take a closer look."

It probably wasn't a good idea, but knowing something was wrong and leaving it alone was like having an itch she couldn't scratch. So while she tackled emptying her side of the storage compartment, Nico worked on the one closest to the kitchenette. "Nothing over here," Greta said. She'd been so sure...

"And I have a mystery button." Nico pressed, and a small door cracked open. He shoved it wider, then grabbed a flashlight from their gear and shone it inside.

It was another compartment—one that sank deeper into the structure of the boat and under part of the kitchenette. It wasn't huge, but definitely bigger than the area beneath the seat, especially with it empty like it was now. At a glance, it was about eight feet long by two and a half feet wide. "I'm guessing it's another storage area, but storage for what? And why keep it hidden like this?"

For a second, Nico shook his head, then he let out a quiet laugh. "I'll be damned." He cast a glance up toward the wheelhouse above them. "Captain Ryan is a smuggler."

"He's a *what*?"

"Relax, Trouble. There's nothing here now, but he obviously has smuggled something at some point. Or the previous owner of the boat did. For all we know, he bought it at auction after it was seized. He might not even know this compartment is here. I'm guessing he does, though, since the coast guard threat was what pushed him to agreeing to take us out."

That didn't make her feel a lot better, but at least it meant they had someplace to stash their stuff if they had to get off the boat. She hadn't wanted to leave her laptop or any other sensitive equipment at the hotel. Better to keep it with them and risk losing it to a potentially unscrupulous boat captain rather than anyone who might break into their room.

Once she reloaded her side of the compartment, she shoved the cushions back in place.

After all the warnings from Marron about the sensitivity of the mission, the threat of a single man seemed less dangerous than that of unknown parties. As safe as they'd been, she knew nothing TRAIT did was ever as safe as it seemed.

Like this mission. She knew *something* was waiting for them in the ocean, but there were more possibilities than she wanted to count. "What do you think we'll find out there?"

Nico shrugged, then wrapped his arms around her, enveloping her in comfort and warmth. "Who knows? Could be anything."

True, but especially since his gut reaction echoed her own, she had a feeling it wasn't going to be anything good. Just like that, she was cold again.

The ship loomed in the distance, directly in their path. There was no question, that floating fortress was their destination, whether Nico liked it or not.

He edged closer to where Greta stood on the bow of the *Salty Sea-Dog*. The wind whipped at the sarong wrapped around her hips, making it fly and giving him a great view of her legs. Much better than looking at the ship in front of them, which was the only thing she seemed to have eyes for at the moment.

He stepped next to her and rested a hand on her back. She leaned into his touch. It was strange how easy touching had become in just two days. There was no flinching, no backing away. There was just the two of them and the sea breeze.

And the mission. "What are you thinking?"

She lowered the binoculars from her eyes and passed them his way. "There hasn't been any movement on deck."

"Maybe everyone's eating or something." He didn't even push any coercion into his voice, and the words still tasted like lies.

"You don't believe that." Greta was getting far too good at reading him—it was disconcerting before they'd had sex. It was kind of terrifying now. "When I say no movement, though, I don't just mean people."

Nico peered through the lenses, shifting his body until he lined up with the ship. She was right. There were no people, but more importantly, not even the fans were spinning. He moved slightly, hunting further. His blood turned to sludge—there wasn't even a flag snapping in the breeze. When the thing had been abandoned, they'd deserted it fully. "It's a ghost ship."

"Yeah."

He couldn't make out the name from this angle, but the USS was clear enough. It was one of theirs. "The military isn't known for abandoning ships to just hang out on the water. I mean, if it sank, that'd be one thing, but why not tug this one in if it just died out here?"

"Because four hundred miles off the coast, in the middle of the Bermuda Triangle, is kind of the perfect place to hide something you don't want found."

Again, she was right. While sailors didn't necessarily *avoid* the area, most weren't exactly fond of going through it if not necessary. It made Nico glance back at the wheelhouse again. Captain Ryan had his teeth clamped on a cigar, and he was steering them on a straight course. He had to see the ship ahead, but he didn't seem to care. The coast guard threat had gotten the man moving, and there'd been no arguments. What was it a man smuggled that would make him do something like this just to avoid detection?

Drug money really didn't seem like a good enough reason.

Nico turned his attention back to the ship, but looking further only led to more questions. There were strange portholes on the side of the ship. Not windows, but actual holes with some sort of covering over them. They looked almost like doors—only without any visible handles. And all of them were shut tight.

"Guess that means it's time to call the boss." Nico reached for the satellite phone in the bag by Greta's feet.

"No." She laid a hand over his just as the boat hit a patch of rough water.

The phone he'd barely wrapped his fingers around flew out of his grip and over the side. "Fuck. Marron's going to have my head."

"No, he won't. It's just a phone." For the first time, Greta seemed less stressed about the mission than he was. "Besides, we had nothing more than confirmation that *something* is here. He's going to want to know what we're dealing with before he'll even consider sending more people. He wants *proof*—and it will have to be more than just the presence of an abandoned military vessel."

"And if we *are* being followed by someone who's involved with the ship—or worse, they have a mole at TRAIT—they'll get wind that we're onto them, and they'll end up moving it." He didn't want to bring up the fact that without the satellite phone, they had absolutely zero means of communication until they were back in range of cell towers.

Greta nodded, the phone seemingly forgotten. "So, we put on our wetsuits and get evidence of whatever's going on now…or we don't get it at all. And this is bigger than one ghost ship hanging out in the Atlantic. It has to be."

He didn't want to argue with her. Calling in the troops seemed the smarter move, but they'd been told to keep as low a profile as possible, and Greta knew Marron would either refuse to send more agents or he'd tell them to back off. If it was the latter, their proof would be gone long before backup arrived, leaving Greta with a dolphin to go with her raccoon. There wasn't anything he could have said to make her agree to a plan that would have that kind of result.

Still, his skin crawled with dread. The ship looked totally deserted, but he couldn't help but feel that there was more to this mess than they could see.

More than anyone was meant to see.

And they were slicing through the water, straight toward it with their eyes wide open.

"I don't think we should get any closer." Captain Ryan gazed up at the *USS Kafka* like it would attack, chomping his pleasure—correction, smuggling—craft in two.

"We paid you to take us there." Like the men, Greta was apprehensive about the ship, but they had to get on board.

"And you said it was a wreck."

They were so close, she could actually feel the damn answers within reach. "Does it look like it's moving anywhere?"

"Lady, that's a military vessel—weird name or not—and I'm not getting arrested for—"

Nico stepped in, his voice going deep as he pushed suggestion into his words. "You don't have to do anything other than get us close enough to grapple our way aboard. Then you can move off and wait for us to signal for pickup. You won't personally be doing anything illegal, *and* you get that nice bonus for getting us back to shore tonight."

The captain frowned, but he steered closer to the dark gray hull of the *Kafka*. "I can get you close, but it looks like someone already took away your access ladders, so good luck getting up there."

There was no arguing with his assessment. The places where ladders had been attached at one point were sheered near smooth. Almost as if even the tiny hand and foot holds that bolts might provide were too much to leave behind. Only the faded paint showed what had once been. Fortunately, they'd come prepared for several possibilities—including something as absurd as this. Greta was just glad they'd also packed the wetsuits, because getting back down wouldn't be nearly as easy as getting up to the deck.

"Steer us as close as you can and kill the engines so we float alongside," Nico said, urging the captain to obey him.

In minutes they were idling next to the *Kafka*. Apparently, the captain really didn't want to risk cutting the engines and being stuck this close to the ship. Considering it was a still-floating military vessel, she was pretty sure their cover story had evaporated, at least with regard to Captain Ryan. There was no way he'd believe this was a treasure hunt of any sort. They'd have to pay him off, but at least it meant the high-tech grappling gun Nico pulled out of their bag wasn't really questioned.

He held it up, brandishing the thing with glee. "Can I say it?" he asked as he wrapped an arm around her waist, pulling her in close enough to kiss, close enough that with fewer clothes, things would have been a very different sort of interesting.

The small bag of essential equipment slung over her shoulder, she wound her arms around him and pressed her lips close to his ear. "Say what?"

Winking, he held her tighter. "I'm Batman." Then he fired the gun, and the hook soared, wrapping over the guardrail until it pulled taut. With the push of another button, the line whirred, lifting both of them from the deck of the *Salty Sea-Dog* straight up to the *Kafka*.

The absence of movement was even eerier here. Nico had called it a ghost ship, but to Greta it was worse than the image that conveyed. Ghost towns at least had the stereotypical tumbleweed blowing through. Here there was nothing, not even a spray of saltwater over the edge.

Instinctively, she reached out and twined her fingers in Nico's. Safety—with him, she was safer.

He looked down at their hands as he unhooked the grappling claw. "You okay?"

She tried to force a smile. "First rule of horror movies is to never split up. I'm just following the rules."

"I always assumed you'd be one of those people who hate horror movies."

"Patterns. They all follow one—it's comforting to only deal with jump scares and not stories that try to defy nature." As they walked from the stern, weapons drawn, she had to let go of him in case of trouble. To distract herself, she started going through the litany of horror tropes.

Go to the place you're warned away from.

Get drunk — at least we skipped that part.

The impure slut dies first. Oh shit. We had sex last night.

Stay together. Just stay together, and you'll be okay.

Because she knew one other thing that was also true about horror movie tropes…it was always a woman who died first. Always.

Chapter Ten

ANYTHING BUT ORDINARY

There was so much about this that Nico didn't like. For starters, there was a system to naming military vessels, and while he recognized the name *Kafka*, it really didn't fit any of the formats. Not that this was a normal ship. During his stint at the army base on Oahu, he'd picked up a thing or two. As best he could tell, this was a research vessel, but it was built like a floating tank.

Nothing topside was locked, and they entered the bridge without issue. Though a layer of dust covered the control panel, light streaming through the windows made streaks in the grime. He and Greta stayed close, within touching distance, almost as if by some unspoken need for contact that neither of them was quite willing to address. "So, when they abandoned the ship, they cut off the ladders, straight to the hull, but they left everything unlocked. It's like they don't care what happens on board."

"They only care that it either stays on board or that

outsiders stay off." Greta frowned at something and stepped away from him, tilting her head to the side in a way that was absurdly adorable. "Nico?"

Following her line of sight, he realized she was examining the dusty control panel. "What is it?"

She waved him over, and he was once again buoyed by her nearness. "Slowly. Don't stir up the air." Once he stood next to her, she pointed. "I thought it was a trick of the light, but do some of these streaks look…different to you?"

Now that he was at this angle, they most definitely did. He knelt down to get a closer look. In several spots, the level of dust was lower, as if it had been scraped bare at some point then re-filled in. It reminded him oddly of the daughter's bedroom in the movie *Interstellar*, where the pattern of the dust had been sending a message. He doubted it was anything that deliberate here. "Someone's been on board since they closed up shop."

"What does that mean?"

"You tell me, pattern girl. Other than a situation like *us*, how does someone end up on a deserted ship? And where are they now?" He really hoped the answer to that was the answer to their whole mystery of what was going on here in the Atlantic. Because with every single creak and groan of the ship, he was waiting for the jump scares that Greta had mentioned. And every second without any only made him more certain one would be coming. He didn't know how to protect her from an unseen threat—and he was determined that they'd make it out of this to go back to Naperville, save the world, and then grow old and cranky together as all good retired spy couples should.

Greta twined her fingers in his and stared at the dust streaks for a long time before saying, "Three options. Whoever deserted the ship came back for some reason. I don't see that as very likely, because it doesn't make sense that they'd come to the bridge again after abandoning the *Kafka*. The logical pattern—and for once, logic is a bit of a stretch—when deserting an area that you want inaccessible is to destroy access, like they did with the ladders. And destroy means of escape. Which would mean the controls were already disabled. Second possibility is someone stumbled on the ship and happened to have gear like we did. Also unlikely because even people who dive for wreckage wouldn't come looking to board something still afloat." She touched the places where the dust was shallower, brow wrinkled in thought.

He wanted to smooth away those lines of worry, but that wouldn't happen until they were safely away from here. "And the third option?"

"Someone was left here intentionally, and they came to the bridge looking for some way to get out." She swept the lines in the dust again. Where the marks had been were engine systems…and communication.

And that made all her horror movie comments sound more likely by the second. "Which means we're not alone."

Greta shrugged, as if that would make the new worry vanish. "Or they've since died. There was still a layer of dust, and since the people who deserted the ship killed the engines and the communications, I'm guessing they didn't exactly leave much in the way of food behind."

It made sense. Patterns, just like she said. The ship wasn't abandoned hastily. Everything was done methodically and with a purpose. But if their mystery person was alive, they were trapped on board and probably not well-informed on the whos, whats, wheres, whens, and hows of all this. Not exactly the bastion of information Nico would have liked on hand. And worse, they could be dangerous. "Okay, so now what?"

"Now we search for something to take back to Marron."

Nico only hoped it wasn't a dead body—or anything worse.

Their search of the deck turned up nothing. As did their subsequent search of the mess hall and the crew quarters. But Greta wasn't fooled. There was no reason to leave a ship out here, floating in the middle of nowhere, with the engines disabled and the ladders removed—unless someone was trying to hide something—but hadn't yet decided to hide it at the bottom of the ocean.

They were about to check out what appeared to be some sort of research command center at the aft of the upper level when a loud clang snagged her attention. Or maybe it was Nico jumping that made her spin around. Either way her focus had shifted to below deck. It seemed his had, too, as he turned and stepped toward the stairs leading into the bowels of the ship. "That sounded bad."

"No. It sounds like evidence." Greta glanced around the command center. Lots of computers and other equipment—good. No people or bodies—even better. She left the door open, knowing this was where she'd likely get most of what Marron would need. The last thing she wanted, though, was for Nico to wander off and get himself in trouble. As much as it would pain her, she'd rather leave with no information as long as it meant he was in one piece when they departed. "We can check out your noise before I dig in here."

They held their weapons at the ready as they edged down the stairs, one on each side. But no one jumped out at them. When they stepped onto the lower deck, Nico said, "What the bloody fuck?"

Greta sucked in a breath and moved closer to him. Contact. Contact meant Nico, and Nico meant security. He'd been at least half right in his assertion, but she didn't think there had been any sex involved in this mess. Both the port and starboard sides of this deck were lined with what looked like crew quarters—only where there should have been walls and doors, these rooms had glass, much of it coated with what looked far too much like dried blood. "I...don't know."

Ever since they'd discovered the coordinates and gotten the mission approved, Greta had pondered what they would find. She expected some sort of data storage. Or perhaps an island too small to be mapped. Or an illegal drilling operation. The ship had been a surprise, but not really. It still fit in her hidden-data idea. But this... What could have happened aboard this ship to leave these rooms—these *cells*—covered in blood?

She walked toward one of the glass partitions and peered inside. Empty. Well, empty of people. There were the remnants of a cot, a smashed sink and toilet, and pictures taped to the walls. She rested her hand against the glass and tried to get a better look. But she jerked away quickly.

The blood was on the outside.

And the inside.

The clanging happened again, louder this time. Greta whipped her head toward the fore. There was a huge hatch in the floor, and someone or something was pounding at it from the other side—from the deck below this one. She nodded at Nico and leveled her weapon at the opening. He knelt down and grabbed the wheel.

Before he moved it so much as an inch, a voice screamed from behind Greta, "No!"

She spun, aiming her weapon at this new threat. What she found hardly fit the definition of the word, though. A woman staggered toward them, her clothing filthy and torn, her hair a bedraggled mess. And the rest of her wasn't faring much better. Skin pulled tight over her bones, making features that had probably once been well-defined seem skeletal. Clearly, she'd been thin before boarding the ship, now...she was gaunt, skin wrinkling over vanishing muscles.

Nico stood, recovering quicker than Greta ever could have, and positioned himself next to her. "Who are you? And what the hell are you doing aboard this ship?"

The woman raked her graying hair back with trembling fingers. "I am Attorney General Patricia Whiddon, and those bastards left me here to die."

Well, that was a bit of a kick in the nuts. As far as Nico knew, Patricia Whiddon was the criminal mastermind behind the attacks on TRAIT and on Senator Carrington's daughter about six months ago. His friend, Finn, had been involved in that mission, and all the evidence had pointed to her. She'd been arrested and charged with conspiracy to commit kidnapping, attempted murder, cyber crimes against the US government, and a bunch of other stuff Nico couldn't recall. She'd used her position to find mercenaries from government ranks willing to attack one of their own, arguably to gain Izzy Carrington and her telekinetic skills as an intelligence asset.

Because of her machinations, Finn had almost lost his job at TRAIT. His partner, and now girlfriend, Jodi Israel, had nearly been killed.

Nico inched closer to Greta. There was no way this woman was bringing them down out here. He wouldn't allow her to take the woman he loved away from him.

But Whiddon didn't move. She just stood there and let out a deep breath.

Was she a threat or not? And if not, what the hell was she doing on the ghost ship of doom that someone had hidden in the middle of the ocean?

More importantly… "Why don't you want me to open the hatch?"

The woman's eyes shifted to the Glock in Greta's hands. "Because I watched the video logs upstairs before I ever came down here. Because I'm terrified they hoped I'd release whatever is down there, and I'd be taken care of in one quick instant of stupidity."

"Videos on the computers upstairs?" Greta asked, her interest perking far more than it had over the banging on the hatch or the discovery of the attorney general's presence.

"Yes." The attorney general sighed as she stepped toward the stairs. "Is the weapon really necessary? I don't have the strength to fight you if I wanted to."

No way was he trusting her without a guard—she'd done enough damage. "Maybe not, but I'd rather not take any chances."

The other woman shrugged and began trudging up the steps. "I don't suppose either of you have any food. They drop rations off once a month, but it's barely enough to survive on."

"No, we don't." Nico frowned. "If you think they want you dead, why are they feeding you?"

She stepped onto the main deck and braced herself against the wall, clearly weak and exhausted. "Maybe they don't *want* me dead so much as they wouldn't be upset if I died. So long as they have plausible deniability, they'll be happy. But I think they're keeping me marginally fed in case they need me again. I can honestly say if you'd shown up with the promise of three squares a day and unlimited water, I might have been willing to say anything you asked me to. Instead you came with guns and reached for that hatch like you had no clue. So I'm guessing the DoD didn't send you to bargain with me."

Nico shot Greta a look. Department of Defense. They'd used Aurora Heights as the random data point that led them here—and a whole lot of people who worked at the Pentagon lived there. It had been a guess based on the damn raccoon and the possibility of a conspiracy theory, but now he had to wonder just how deep that rabbit hole went. How close had she gotten when that animal had thrown them off the scent? "Show us the logs."

The attorney general moved into the command center and collapsed on a chair with a grateful exhale. She punched a few commands into the computer. "I'm honestly surprised they didn't destroy these when they deserted the ship, but I guess they didn't want to lose the data entirely. For all I know, they hoped to replicate the experiments to better success." Pages and pages of numbers popped up, as well as official reports, but Whiddon skipped over all of those. "To answer the question of what is down below, you just need to watch the video logs. Do you want to start at the beginning or jump to the ugly truth?"

Greta swallowed hard. "One of the early ones, and then whatever it is we *must* know."

Nico kept his gun trained on the attorney general but placed his other hand on the small of Greta's back. Whether or not she needed the touch, he had a feeling he would. Hell, he was pretty sure before all this was over, he was going to need more than just this.

Whiddon pulled the first file up, and they fell silent.

The camera focused on a grinning man in a white lab coat. Bald head, a bit of extra padding around his face, little circle glasses around bright blue eyes. His nametag said Dr. Brougham. "January second, 2014."

"That's almost two years ago," Nico said, his voice quiet. "This ship has been out here all that time?"

Greta shushed him. The answers they needed were here, and while he might be nervous about discovering what they were, she needed to know. *They* needed to know.

On the screen, Dr. Brougham continued, "It's the first

day of trials, and everyone is recovered from their New Years' hangover and extremely excited. The initial injections were given this morning, and already we're seeing slight changes. Lowered heart rates—approaching those of professional athletes. Increased metabolism, at least if the subjects' appetites are any indication. We did baseline strength testing yesterday, but we won't measure that again until tomorrow. I will say, though, that all early signs are positive, and the men are in good spirits. I'm sure the bonuses have something to do with that, but it's better than starting with them all cranky. They're already taking bets on who'll get the title of Captain America. When I mentioned legal issues, they laughed it off, saying Marvel could hardly argue if we make their fiction a reality."

The video ran out as something in the background clattered to the floor, and Dr. Brougham let out a muffled curse. Nico ran the back of his hand across his mouth. "The US government was running super-soldier research? Are you sure this isn't a hoax?"

He wanted it to be a hoax.

He'd seen the movies. He'd read the comics. There were reasons craziness like this wasn't a reality—namely the myriad of ways it could go wrong. But with all the weird reality TRAIT had faced in the last few years, he couldn't summon enough hope to really believe it was fake.

"From what I could digest of the reading material available, they're utilizing some sort of chromosomal reshuffling with certain genes from different animals, but I really don't understand the science. As for the rest, you tell me." Whiddon clicked on another file.

Dr. Brougham was on screen again, looking much more haggard. His glasses were slightly askew, and there was a streak of crimson on his lab coat. "April twenty-first, 2014. We brought Talcott out today after he sliced up his knuckles banging on the glass. He became agitated before we even opened the door, so we were forced to utilize the tranq gun in order to subdue him and get him into the exam room. He's currently on the table, and his vitals are all well within acceptable range. Brain activity is…strange. He seems to be going through spurts of incredibly intense activity followed by near shutdown of all function. I've never seen anything like it. We're going to attempt to attach electrodes so we can monitor him more closely and determine if the outbursts are aligning with the activity spikes. At this point, I am strongly recommending shutting down the program entirely until we ascertain…"

Off screen, a panicked voice said, "Doctor Brougham. Doctor! He's waking up!"

The doctor spun from the screen and bolted from his chair just as a scream echoed through the speakers. His lab coat caught on something and yanked open, revealing a Beretta in a holster under his arm. "Talcott, calm down. No one here is going to hurt you."

Another scream as a woman's body in a bloody lab coat was flung across the room. It hit the wall with bone-jarring force, and then a shirtless man with rippling muscles pounced on the body, yanking the unconscious form upright. The man buried his face in her neck like he was trying to make out with her, but when he yanked his head back, a bloody chunk of skin and muscle was caught between his teeth.

A gunshot rang out, and the man's body jerked but didn't fall. Another gunshot. Still, he was upright, his mouth buried in the woman's flesh. The last bullet hit the back of his head; blood and brain matter sprayed across the wall. His body sagged against the woman's, and both slid to the floor.

It was a long minute before Dr. Brougham sat down in front of the camera again. He blinked, as if trying to remember what he was doing, then said, "Staff Sergeant Talcott was eliminated from the program at fourteen-twenty hours on April twenty-first, 2014. Needless to say, brain monitoring is no longer an option. Reiterating recommendation to shut down the program until we determine the cause behind the violent outbursts. I will await further orders in this regard."

The screen went dead.

"Violent outbursts? They're calling that a *violent outburst*?" Nico said, staring at the screen. While they'd watched, he'd tightened his grip on both his weapon and on Greta. She didn't appear to notice, standing there in what seemed as much shock as he was. The US government had tried to create super-soldiers and wound up with a horde of would-be zombies. No wonder the ship and its murderous cargo were stashed out here.

Whiddon nodded, her finger hovering over another icon. "There's more if you want to see it, but from what I've been able to work through, before I was disgusted enough to stop watching, the lower level? That's where the last of the test subjects are."

"What are they eating?" Nico asked, not really wanting to know.

"Each other? Maybe the DoD has a way to siphon food directly to that level when they drop off the rations they keep leaving me. I don't know. I don't care. But if we open that hatch, I'm afraid what we'll find is they haven't been fed at all."

And a swarm of hungry zombies was *not* something they needed right now. "Greta?"

As if zombie-super-soldiers had actually been on her list of possibilities when they came aboard—and considering the aliens and dragons, for all he knew, it might have been— she calmly reached into the inner pocket of her wetsuit and withdrew a small storage drive Jodi had designed and shoved it into the USB port. "We take it all. We take it back to Marron, and he can figure out what to do with it."

The attorney general's spine straightened, like that announcement was the thing that suddenly gave her strength. "You're TRAIT?"

Greta nodded. "Agents Gallagher and Tancredi."

"You need to leave. Now. If they have any idea you're here—" Whiddon shut up, and Nico caught the same sound she must have. A boat—small and fast—approaching far more quickly than they could get Captain Ryan back for a pickup. "Too late. They're here. We're all dead."

It was a strange world indeed when zombies had suddenly become the least of their problems.

Chapter Eleven

EVERYTHING IS NOT WHAT IT SEEMS

Greta had shifted all the files, but with so much video, it was taking forever to finish loading. And with trouble on the way, they needed as many answers as they could get. They'd almost lost Jodi to Whiddon's treachery. Greta really didn't want to talk to her, but she was their only source of intel here. "As far as we knew, the DoD had you in protective custody after you were arrested. Why throw you out here for what you did?"

Whiddon snorted. "That's just it, dear girl. *I* didn't do anything, but I can't prove it from the middle of the Atlantic, if I could have proven it at all. Obviously, I was set up to take the fall for another of the DoD's ridiculous ploys, and with how well it was orchestrated, the plan came from high up the food chain, possibly from the top. That's why it was so easy for your friends at TRAIT to buy into it hook, line, and sinker."

Finn and Jodi had both come to that conclusion about her immediately: she was the guilty party with means, motive, and opportunity. She had just found out about TRAIT, but she seemed to hate the agency without even knowing about their work. She insisted her own people handle the security at Senator Carrington's home...the list of evidence against her had been perfect. She had the means of executing the kidnapping attempt via recruiting from her own people. It was a simple motive of discounting the competition to put herself and her people in higher esteem, as well as grabbing Izzy Carrington as an asset. Opportunity presented itself through the entire setup at Carrington's place. *Everything* had presented itself nice and neat and orderly. A seemingly perfect pattern.

And that was its flaw. It was too perfect. It was perfect by design rather than by the natural order of things. Greta should have recognized it right off.

The worst part—now she was starting to see how Izzy Carrington and her abilities, as well as discrediting the attorney general, would fit into a larger plan. She didn't have all the pieces yet, but they had to get out of here and back to TRAIT.

Nico stepped inside the room again, touching her, soothing away her worries, if only for a moment. She'd brought him into this mess. She'd insisted they investigate. If he died out here, it would be on her. "The ship that's coming isn't big, but somehow that's actually making me feel worse about our chances of getting out of here." He glanced back over his shoulder. "We have about a minute before they arrive."

And the three of them had a couple semiautomatics for defense. And a bunch of violent super-soldiers in the hold. Great.

What would Buffy do?

For starters, she would have killed the monsters.

But Greta had always been more Willow than Buffy— only without the badass witch powers. So the better question was… What would nerdy, season-one Willow do?

"She'd grab Xander and get the hell out of the way," Greta muttered. That wasn't really an option. Not when they didn't have a Buffy to deal with everything else. But she definitely needed to get her crush out of this. There was no other option.

Greta's head snapped up. They didn't have a Buffy, but they might have something even better. She had her Xander. "Nico, can you do your thing? Talk to them?"

He leaned against the doorjamb and blew out a deep breath. "I can try, but I'm going to be honest, I'll probably get shot. Like I told you—it isn't magic; it's just convincing people of stuff they kind of want to do or believe anyway."

"Well, if nothing else, I need you to stall them. We need these files if we do manage to get out of this alive."

"Got it." He ducked back out the door.

"Try *not* to get shot. I fully intend on both of us making it home."

Whiddon pushed up from the chair. "What can I do to help?"

Nothing? Greta knew that wasn't what she was supposed to say, though. In times of crisis, people didn't want the truth. They wanted reassurance that everything would be okay.

She wasn't good at that sort of thing. "You just need to try not to die, too."

After all…if each and every one of them managed that, it would be a miracle.

Too bad miracles totally didn't follow any pattern she knew.

The speedboat pulled up about ten yards off the *Kafka's* starboard side. Nico could probably hit someone from here, considering he had the high ground—such as it was—but he had a feeling the men on the boat had a lot more firepower than he did, even with a couple extra magazines in his pocket.

Greta had told him to stall, though, and shooting at them wouldn't accomplish that. So, against his better judgment, he holstered his weapon…and waved at the boat. "Damn, am I glad to see you guys."

The men on the boat glanced at each other, their expressions wary. Wary was okay. He could work with that.

"We've been trying to get this hunk of junk moving, but it's totally dead. So I went below to get to the engine room, but the hatch is locked down tight. Maybe you could come aboard and help us out with that?" He waved back toward the ship's interior, praying Greta didn't come out. He wanted her safe, and for the moment, inside was safe.

One of the men picked up a bullhorn and spoke into it. "The engine room isn't down there, but we're pretty sure you already figured that out, Agent Tancredi."

It was so not encouraging that the bad guys knew his name. "Are you sure? That's where all the clanging noises came from. Maybe if you could at least toss up some WD-40 I can figure out what's making the damn noise. It's harder than hell to concentrate with all that racket."

When they didn't bite, he tried a slightly different tactic. "Come on, help a guy out. I brought my girl all the way out here for a little adventure time, if you know what I mean." He made a point to raise his eyebrow suggestively, even though he was confident they couldn't see it from where they stood. "She's freaking out about the noise, and I've got to admit, it's even killing my boner. So I'd really like to make it stop."

A giant man with a shaved head and stern expression grabbed the bullhorn. He looked like Roadblock from *GI Joe*, only minus the southern charm. "Stay away from the hatch, agent. That's an order."

They're afraid of the zombies.

Granted, from what he'd seen on the video, they should be, but he hadn't expected them to be quite so open about it. Unfortunately, they didn't seem to be playing along. Time to switch the game up a little. Releasing the attitude in three... two...one...

"First, I'm not in the army anymore, and you really don't look like my boss, so orders are null and void, big guy, but thanks for playing."

"If you let those things out, you're going to die. Do you have a death wish, agent?"

No, but he was starting to have a plan—one that would get all of them out of this alive—and that was a vast improvement from a few seconds ago. Then a horrible thought hit him—more like a few horrible thoughts. The dolphins. The kids who walked the beach on their way home from school. The missing bath salts murderer... All of it in the months right after Dr. Brougham had killed Talcott. "Holy crap. You idiots let one get away, didn't you?"

"That's none of your concern, agent. Now get your partner, and we can discuss the charges against you on the way back to Florida." Roadblock crossed massive arms over his chest, like he was done discussing the whole matter.

Nico wasn't, not by a long shot—especially now that the guy had brought Greta into the mix. Those assholes were *not* getting their hands on her, not if he had any way to stop it. "So...you let a fucking zombie loose in Miami, and you're worried about the crimes *I've* committed? Pretty sure the Snickers bar I nicked from Seven-Eleven when I was twelve didn't kill anyone. And the time I skinny-dipped in the city pool didn't involve the vicious slaughter of a couple dolphins."

"The subject in question has been eliminated. While the civilian casualties were tragic, they were unavoidable. I would prefer you and Agent Gallagher were not added to the list of *unavoidable incidents*. We have a hook ladder here. You will get your partner and join us immediately."

"Yeah. I hate to tell you, but she's kind of stubborn. Only child and all that. You're probably going to have to come up and convince her yourself." Time. Greta just needed a little more time…

"None of my men are boarding that ship. So you have two choices: follow my instructions to the letter or die. Do I make myself clear?"

"Crystal." Their time was up. Roadblock wasn't going to put up with many more of Nico's shenanigans, and there wasn't a chance in hell his ability would work on these guys. They were under orders, and they were more than happy to follow them. Convincing them to simply let their targets go wasn't an option. He'd suspected as much before they started talking, but after the first words, he knew without a doubt.

They were fucked…in the ass…with a two-by-four.

"Hey, sweetheart," he called over his shoulder, hoping Greta was almost done, "the boys are insisting we join them for dinner. Need me to grab anything before we go?"

*S*weetheart?

Oh. That was a warning from Nico that they were out of time. She smiled. It was nice to hear him call her that, even though she'd grown to like "Trouble" more. Greta glanced at the computer. Thirty seconds, and they'd have all the files… and no way to get back to TRAIT. Not only was their ride hanging out at least a hundred yards away from the ship—if the men in the speedboat hadn't disabled or destroyed it— but it wasn't fast enough to outrun their enemies even if they were able to get on board.

"Yes, honey," she said, embracing the novelty of the pet names. "I need you to grab an escape plan."

"What was that?" he yelled. She was about to repeat herself when Nico continued, hollering at the people in the other boat, "Women. I swear. Be right back, guys."

Seconds later he was by her side, and the transfer was complete. She detached the drive and shoved it inside a pocket of her wetsuit. "Got a plan?"

"Your man will always provide for you. Though, in this case, I'm providing zombies."

"What?" Greta and Whiddon said at the same time. He was clearly crazy. Wonderful, amazing, and sexy—but crazy.

Nico held up his hands. "The guys down there are terrified of them."

"So am *I*," Greta pointed out. "You should be, too."

"I am, but if they're distracted with the zombies, *we* have a chance to get out of here alive. From the sounds of things, they aren't only under orders to nab us—they're planning to hide the *Kafka* better, at the bottom of the ocean."

"What makes you so sure?"

"They said they weren't boarding, but we were dead if we didn't go with them. They can't shoot us from down there, and they have no reason to believe we don't have a way to contact TRAIT—which we would have had if our sat phone hadn't gone overboard. So logic says they must have some means to destroy the ship. Which means, our plan is to send them into a panic long enough to buy us a little time."

"How? We have two Glocks and no clue how many men are in the hold. We can't even pretend to know how they'll behave. We—"

Attorney General Whiddon grabbed Greta's flailing hands and held them still. "You two are going to go to the far side of the ship, signal your rescue, and jump into the water. Someone is making it off this infernal ship and back to the mainland. *Someone* needs to make sure the proper people know what happened out here. And that person can't be me.

I'm too weak—I won't even make it to your boat. Which means I'll release the test subjects."

"You can't," Greta argued, pulling the woman to her feet. "You need to get back and clear your name."

"You're going to do that for me. I can't swim to the boat; I don't have the strength. In a fight...I'm useless. But I will make the very best bait ever." She sank back into the chair and spun toward the computer, sliding files out of the way until she came to one labeled *Security Systems*. Inside, she hovered over something that said *Latch Release*. "I might be wrong about what this does, but in thirty seconds, I'm pushing this button. I would suggest you are as far away from here as possible."

Nico snapped to attention and saluted. "Yes, ma'am. We won't forget this."

Greta knew she should do something...say something. Marissa or Penelope would have hugged the woman, but it would have felt fake coming from her. So she said the only words she had for a situation where someone did a selfless act for her benefit. "Thank you." It wasn't enough, not by a long shot. "I...I don't know what else to say."

Whiddon gave a wan smile. "Just make sure the world knows the truth. And get the bastards who put us all through this." Her gaze darted to the stairs and the hatch in the floor, her mind obviously thinking of the men trapped behind the hatch. "All of us."

Greta nodded curtly, and then they were gone—out the opposite door and racing down the deck, stowing their weapons within the waterproof pockets of their wetsuits. There was nothing left in her bag of goodies that would be irreparably damaged by a dunking, so she left it as it was. Greta counted all the while they ran, but she needn't have bothered. The moment the subjects were released from their prison wasn't one that could be missed. Nor could Patricia

Whiddon's screams.

The *Salty Sea-Dog* sat farther off than expected, but they could make it if the others were distracted by the trouble aboard the *Kafka*. Nico flashed his signal light at the boat, but from this far away, it was impossible to tell if it had started motoring toward them or not. "Jump now?"

Greta risked a glance behind her, hoping she couldn't see the source of the unholy noises. But then one of the super-soldiers rounded the corner. Greta wanted to be gone before they were spotted. "Do we have a choice?" Before it headed their way, she grabbed Nico's hand and they took a running leap off the ship.

She expected to fall into the water, but a concussive blast sounded and then a wall of heated air pushed her further over the ocean. When she hit the surface, she forgot…everything.

Chapter Twelve

NOT LIKE THE MOVIES

Greta woke in darkness. At least she thought she was awake. She hurt all over, so it seemed unlikely she was dead. The instant a groan started to escape her lips though, a hand slapped over her mouth.

"You have to be quiet. One of them is on board."

Nico. He was alive. She recognized his whisper immediately and nodded. He shifted his hand away, and she very carefully rolled toward him. "Super-soldier?"

"Military. At least that's my guess."

She heard footsteps and quieted, trying to figure out what happened and where they were. At least it wasn't a cell of any sort—that was good enough for the moment, all things considered. They'd jumped off the ship, and then…there was an explosion? As soon as the noise above quieted, she asked, "Did they blow the ship?"

"Yeah. I was right about the sinking thing. Apparently keeping the zombies alive was only a priority so long as they were locked up tight."

She had a hard time believing it was as simple as that. An engine rumbled to life beneath them, and she shifted closer, reveling in him and the fact they'd even made it this far—especially with her unconscious. "Where are we anyway?"

"Remember Captain Ryan's secret smuggling compartments? We're in one. When I found him dead on board, I knew they'd come back for the boat. So I dried off the deck after I dragged us out of the water, but this was the only place I could think of to hide."

If they left no obvious traces from getting aboard, it would be assumed they died in the explosion or in the water. All they had to do was take care of their new friend in the wheelhouse. Then they could make it to shore, grab their car, and be back to Naperville by nightfall tomorrow. She could hand all of this mess off to Marron, leaving her and Nico time to get to know each other—for real. "It was a good choice. If there's only one of them aboard…"

The thought trailed off as she realized the answer, but Nico said it anyway, "We kill him, and they know we're alive for sure. They won't stop hunting us until we're fucking buried. If we stay hidden, we might still get out of this alive—at least long enough to get the files back to TRAIT. I just wish I could figure out why they're moving us."

It only took seconds for Greta to connect the dots in her mind. "Captain Ryan works for people—both smuggling and likely for charters, too. If the boat goes missing, and he doesn't check in, people will look for it. GPS, or even if he called in a general sailing plan once we were on board. If people come looking out here too soon, they might find the *Kafka*. Better to move Ryan's boat at least a short distance away."

"And his body?"

Greta didn't want to think about the body, so she clung to Nico and shook her head against his chest. Captain Ryan had been a little surly and a smuggler of…something, but he hadn't deserved to get messed up in all this.

The noise from the engine was loud but soothing. If they didn't do something to stay awake, they would likely both pass out, and their snoring would alert someone when the boat stopped. Nico shifted, and his leg pressed between her thighs. She bit her lip, remembering his hands and mouth on her, remembering him thrusting into her with abandon. "I wish we'd thought to smuggle condoms with us."

He buried his face in her hair as he laughed, his knee doing the most terrible, wonderful things to her in the process. "Trouble, where the hell do you think I stashed our stuff when we hit the *Kafka*?"

She frowned as something poked against her back, but the expression disappeared as she wriggled closer to Nico. "We can't have sex while the bad guy is taking us who knows where. If we do that, we deserve to die."

"I know, but I also figured you wouldn't mind knowing that not only is your laptop safe, we also *can* have sex if and when we get out of this."

Greta laughed softly, burying her head in his neck and muffling the sound even more. "Thank you."

"For saving your laptop or for the condoms? Because those involve two very different kinds of 'you're welcome,' one of which we just agreed we couldn't do here."

This time the laughter lasted longer. On the *Kafka*, Greta had feared she might never laugh again. If she'd had to go through this alone…if she'd made it but he hadn't, or worse, if she'd never had him at all… The thought sobered her immediately. They *had* both survived, and no matter what, they were finishing the mission so they could explore this new relationship.

But that meant staying alert, regardless of the rocking of the boat or the oddly soothing rumble of the engine. Greta pulled back. "We need to keep each other awake."

"I thought you said no sex." She could almost feel the sarcasm in his voice.

"Thanks for laying it on so thick I couldn't miss it in the dark. What I meant is we need to talk about something other than sex or one of two things will happen. One: we'll fall asleep. Two: we'll prove we're too stupid to live and get shot."

Nico squirmed a few inches away. "I think I can reach the bag and at least give us a tiny bit of light. That should help with the not sleeping, too."

He flicked on one of the headlamps they'd brought along, casting the space in a dim glow. Looking around the tight space, Greta took in things she hadn't noticed during their cursory glance earlier. The compartment hadn't been empty after all.

The light caught on something reflecting back at her. She took the headlamp and directed the glow that way. Tucked into a corner was a very worn stuffed bear. It was small, the kind of thing even a child could hold in one hand. She reached out and drew it toward them. Stitched into the fur was a name: Sofia. It was well-loved like the bunny in *The Velveteen Rabbit*, not the type of thing a child left behind voluntarily.

Holding her breath, Greta shined the light on all the other crevices. A pacifier. A lock of dark hair caught on a piece of wood. A handkerchief.

"He smuggled people." Not drugs. Not cigars. People. That's why the compartment was the perfect size for the two of them to hide in. You could even fit more if necessary. Greta suddenly couldn't get any air.

Nico pulled her close and took the light away. "Breathe, Trouble. I've got you." The glow met the ceiling of the compartment, and he said, "Look."

On the ceiling were drawings, like it was some sort of ancient cave, only decorated in crayons and marker rather than dirt and spit. Smiley faces, happy suns, and the largest: a grinning stick-family, stepping off a boat near a sketch of Florida. "Not the slave trade."

"No. My guess is he smuggled refugees."

Greta held Sofia's bear, wondering again how it wound up left behind. "And these things?"

"The passengers were caught before they left their own country? They had to rush off Ryan's boat when they made landfall here? There could be all sorts of reasons."

"They could have died…" A sob caught in her throat as she clutched the threadbare teddy. The families, the children, could have died, just like she and Nico could have. How they might still.

"Maybe, but probably not. They're most likely safe and sound and the kid has a brand new stuffed animal." Nico pried the bear from her grasp. "This guy? He's part of her past—part of her old life. And now he's here, standing sentinel over everyone else who sneaks a ride in this compartment—including us."

When she finally thought she could speak without sobbing, she reached out and ran her fingers along what was left of the bear's fur. "I'm glad he's protecting us then, because the most unfair part of dying out here would be that I've waited too long to find you."

He covered her mouth with his, but she still kept silently thanking whatever force had saved them from anything more than bumps and bruises. She thanked Captain Ryan for having this compartment. She thanked little Sofia—wherever she was—for leaving her bear behind.

The way Greta was…her family had convinced her that no one would ever really understand her, that she'd be alone forever. And then Nico walked into her office and wound up staying. She'd never dared hope for someone like him. Someone who *saw* her and stuck around instead of running away.

"Hey," he said, drawing back, "don't disappear on me. I know this is all a mess and you need something to pour your energy into, but for right now, I'm your top. You don't need to stress out. You don't need to spin. You just need me."

And she did. She needed Nico like she needed to breathe. She'd been living without air for far too long. Even if she died today, she was going out knowing exactly how full her lungs and life could be.

"Now. I need you now and always."

He'd lived so he could hear those words fall from Greta's lips. Damn, it felt good. But her mouth on his made it feel even better. For the longest time, they stayed like that, holding each other, mouths barely separated, breathing the same air as their hearts pounded in time to a slowing engine.

Shit. Had they made too much noise while talking about the other people? Had the light been visible somehow? "Why are we stopping?"

Greta was silent for a moment. "We haven't gone far enough to be back to shore, not even at top speed. An hour at most, probably not even that."

"Should I get our weapons?" Nico reached for the bag.

Her fingers on his arm stilled his movement. "Slow and quiet. Logically, if he heard us, he would have cut the engines immediately. Element of surprise and all that."

It only took a few seconds to grab their Glocks, but he really wished they'd thought to bring more weapons. When the compartment opened, the sun would be blinding to them after so much darkness—even with the headlamp's glow.

But no one rushed around overhead. No one threatened their hiding spot. Soon enough, the engine *did* cut off, and the sound of another boat rumbled quietly through the hull.

Now footsteps tromped on the deck, sounding as if something was being dragged behind. The man up top yelled, "What about the blood?"

Someone else yelled back, "Leave it and chum the water. By the time anyone finds him or the boat, it'll just look like he tried to pull himself aboard again."

Captain Ryan. They were feeding his body to the sharks and dumping the boat here…wherever here was. On a high note, it meant they weren't blowing it up. He and Greta would live. Low note, the men could plan to disable the engines as some sort of ruse that would explain the captain going over. At least there was no excuse to kill the radio.

Minutes later, the other boat sped away, and there were no more noises from the deck. Nico's muscles relaxed, and he gathered Greta to him. "I'm totally deferring to your logic on this, Trouble. Stay or move?"

Greta blew out a slow breath. "Stay. For now. Long enough to make sure no one was left on board—in case they suspected we did something like this."

"Okay." He held her tight, breathing in the scent of her, savoring the feel of her skin against his without the fear it might be the last time. His gut said the men were gone, but he wasn't about to give up time clinging to her and celebrating the fact that they'd made it out of this alive.

They stayed hidden somewhere between thirty minutes and an hour before Greta disentangled herself from Nico's arms and agreed that they could come out. Several sharks circled the boat, but no sign of Captain Ryan remained other than a slight stain to the water and scraps of clothing. Thankfully, there was also no sign of the men who had blown up the *Kafka*.

Desperate to get off the water and somewhere safer, she tipped her head toward the wheelhouse and said, "Do you know how to work any of this? Figure out where we are and maybe get us back to shore?"

Nico shrugged. "My parents had a boat when I was a kid, so I shouldn't get us killed steering, but the rest is iffy. What are you going to do while I rescue us from sharks?"

She dragged her laptop out of their bag of gear and sat down. "I'm going to look at all our new data and formulate a plan to survive long enough to get back to TRAIT."

"Why was I afraid you were going to say it wasn't over?"

"Because you aren't an idiot."

"And I pride myself on that fact every day, so thank you for noticing." He kissed her briefly, just a gentle brush against lips bruised from their interlude in the smuggling compartment. "What about sending something to Marron once we make landfall?"

"I've been thinking about that, and if it really is the DoD—which we have no reason not to believe at this point—I worry they have someone on the inside at TRAIT, or at the very least a way to monitor communications, which is probably the more likely alternative." Maybe they could code something, but she hadn't yet figured out a way to do it that wouldn't be noticed.

"I'll ponder a way to sneak something through while I drive." It was like they were already becoming one of those couples who finished each other's thoughts. The idea made Greta let out a happy sigh as Nico turned toward the wheelhouse. "Get to work, and try to keep an eye on our aft, make sure we don't pick up a tail of any sort."

"Aye aye, Captain." After giving herself a minute to watch Nico's ass while he walked away, she booted up the laptop. Granted, everything was stored in her brain, but at the moment, she was having trouble seeing the forest for the trees—largely because she'd never seen a forest with so many different kinds of trees in one spot before.

The engines started easily, and before the computer even fully booted, Nico had them on their way, which meant she could turn her focus to her own tasks without too much worry.

Back at TRAIT, she'd have all her monitors and be able to do things much more efficiently, but here she was limited by one small screen, the rocking of the boat, and the need to keep an eye on the ocean at their backs. So instead of anything fancy, she pulled up a simple Word doc that listed all the data they had. To the schoolchildren's deaths and the ravaged dolphins she added: *super-soldiers, Attorney General Whiddon,* and *military connection.*

With that done, she started adding details. Where the kids disappeared. Where the dolphins were found. The location of the *Kafka.* A note to double-check the case that had led to Whiddon's capture. The fact that she and Nico had been followed, not only to Florida but to the boat.

She jerked away from the laptop. Maybe the DoD knew where they were going because of a bug or plant at TRAIT, but there was also a chance they themselves had been tagged. Greta tore through their bag, itemizing which things had been in their possession since leaving TRAIT and which had been out of sight at some point. If they'd been followed from Illinois, the tracker had been placed there. But guarantees in their line of work were few, and Greta didn't think the *exact same* people Nico had seen outside the apartment had been the ones at the *Kafka.*

No. It was more likely, based on their readiness to blow the ship, that those men had been stationed here, watching. Which meant communication from someone else. Likely monitoring from somewhere else.

She rushed back to where they'd holed up and grabbed

the towel. She ran her hands over the seams and every inch of the weave. Nothing. Busting open the case from Nico's sunglasses didn't give her anything, either. She'd poured the sunscreen onto the deck, hunting inside the bottle and out. Nothing.

The equipment they'd been supplied at TRAIT was equally free of any tampering. Had it been the grappling gun? They'd left that on the *Kafka*. She thought back to the gun. No, especially for anyone who knew where they were going, that would be the least logical place to hide a tracker.

But they *were* being tracked. They had to be. Odds were it wasn't precise enough to tell the difference between its location on the *Salty Sea-Dog* when they'd actually been on the *Kafka*, but even if they figured out it had been left here, the fact that it was moving again would show up soon enough.

And that meant she had to ditch the tracker or the people after them would know they were still alive. But so far, she'd come up empty. Had they really been tagged way back at TRAIT? There had been whispers of a turncoat agent once upon a time, but she'd never believed them—until now. What else had come with them?

Her gaze swept over her laptop and all their tech gear. How would she even find a tracker in all that? Then her eyes fell on the bag itself.

"Damn it." She whipped the canvas off the ground and turned it inside out. There. *Right there*, tucked into one of the seams. She tore it free and threw it overboard. The salt water would kill the signal soon enough. Hopefully no one had looked at its status after finding them. *Hopefully* they would think she or Nico had the bag with them onboard the *Kafka*, and that's why the signal died. If not, the fact that they'd survived was no longer a secret.

Having disposed of the tracker, she put everything back in the bag, picked up her laptop again, and typed the words "agents assumed dead" at the bottom of the list. If the enemy knew they were alive, it changed everything, but it also meant they'd probably never make landfall.

Dead, however, she and Nico had a chance to get the information back to TRAIT. Dead, they had a chance of bringing down the people involved. Dead, they had a chance of surviving.

Greta made Nico drive up the coast a bit and ditch the boat near Ft. Lauderdale. Apparently they weren't going back to their rental car, much less back to the hotel for their things. It made sense, but Nico was glad he hadn't brought anything he wouldn't want to lose with him.

Except Greta. He'd brought her, and there was no way *anything* he might have left behind in Miami was worth risking her again.

A quick look at cash on hand made it clear they weren't going to be getting back to Illinois by any legal means. He'd only kept enough on him to pay off Captain Ryan. They might have been able to rent a car…tomorrow, but that would require their fake IDs, which he no longer had. Luckily, he had a plan B.

With darkness making them little more than shadows, they made their way on foot to the nearest car dealership. Most of the staff had already left, but Nico managed to tag the last salesman to walk out the door.

"Sir, I'm sorry to bother you. I know you're closed for the night, but I really need your help." He stuck his foot in the door before it latched shut.

The guy eyeballed the obstruction and said, "Son, don't make me call the authorities."

Time to see if his specialty was really worth anything in

the field when push came to shove. "That's the thing," Nico said, flashing his badge too fast for the man to see anything, "I *am* the authorities, and I need to commandeer your vehicle."

"You need to what?"

"It's a matter of national security. I know you can take home a rental or a test drive tonight. We need something that won't be missed by anyone but you. We'll make sure you are compensated for this inconvenience *and* given the recognition you deserve for helping your government in its time of need." The guy was rubbing his chin, clearly on the hook. Nico just needed to reel him in. Time to weave in some fabricated facts to drive the point home. "If we make it back in time to stop this attack, you'll be a hero."

"And if you wreck my car?"

"As I mentioned, you'll be compensated in full, either monetarily or with a new vehicle." *Come on, buddy, we're in a bit of a time crunch. Bad guys and all that crap…*

"Are you protecting the blonde? She reminds me of my daughter."

The blonde… Oh. Greta. He'd told her to stay back since this was going to be an iffy deal anyway, but obviously the salesman had caught sight of her. "Yes, sir, I am. It's imperative I get her to Chicago as quietly as possible. Our fate is in her hands, and her fate is in mine. Will you help us?"

The man dropped a set of keys into Nico's hand. "I'll help her. White Honda Civic to your left." He grabbed the door, ready to go in and snag an overnight vehicle. "Keep her safe, son."

"I will, but please remember, not a word of this to anyone."

"Understood." The man handed him a card that Nico immediately tucked away and disappeared into the darkness of the dealership.

Nico waved Greta over and raced toward the Civic before their new friend had a change of heart. There was a mountain of empty coffee cups in the back, but at least it had a full tank of gas. Greta collapsed into the passenger seat, and as soon as she had her door shut, they pulled from the lot. A quick stop to grab food from a drive-thru and they were on their way, the in-dash navigation system programmed to take them back to Illinois.

"How do you want to play this? Drive straight through? Do we have enough cash for a hotel room?" He kind of hoped they did. Even if the place was seedy as fuck, they both smelled like dead fish. It was going to get old quickly.

Greta shook her head. "Cash, probably, but we don't have the time. The person or people doing this *know* that we were at the *Kafka*. Even if they think we're dead, everything is telling me that time is of the essence." Her nose wrinkled. "If you find a truck stop with showers, though, we could probably spare a little break for that."

And the people doing all this also knew they were with TRAIT. They'd called him out by name as soon as he showed himself. "What about Marron?"

"There are too many variables—including the possibility that the office communications have been compromised like I mentioned. I still haven't figured out a way to encode a message that won't tip off outsiders."

Nico nodded. He'd been toying with an idea on the boat, but he needed time. "Figure out the most imperative information to get to him. I have a plan, but it's going to take some thought, and the fewer words we have to get to him, the better."

"I can do that." She stared at the list on her laptop and started typing a new, shorter one. "You were great back there with the salesman by the way. I couldn't do this… I couldn't be in the field without you."

Coming from Greta, that was praise of the highest order. "Ditto, Trouble. We work well together, and not just in bed."

"Yeah, but I really did like the bed." She gave him a shy smile, her dimple barely peeking out, and he reached over to caress her thigh. "If we only slightly bend speed laws and don't make too many stops, we can be at the office by midday. So long as they think we're dead, the DoD has time to formulate a plan before they do anything to TRAIT. *If* they do anything to TRAIT."

"What do you mean, *if?*"

Greta stifled a yawn. "I'm not sure what I mean, but they know about us. Which means if they wanted to hit us, they would have already."

"You mean like the crew who went after Jodi and Finn in the spring?"

"I don't know. Right now it's like I can see the pattern, but I can't grab hold of it."

Finally on I-95, Nico set the cruise control and let himself focus on Greta for a second. Sagging in the seat, she'd barely touched her French fries, much less the burger in her lap. She was dead on her feet, possibly with a concussion from the explosion. They both needed rest, but how the hell was he supposed to let her drive when her turn came?

He reached out and brushed a loose strand of hair off her cheek. She'd been awake for a few hours since the explosion though, and acting perfectly normal. At least that meant he could let her sleep. "Eat your food and crash for a while. I'll ponder the code and wake you once we hit a good stop."

"Or if you're too tired to drive," she said, hand covering her mouth as she tried to talk through her yawn.

"Or that."

But by the time the words were out of his mouth, she was already passed out, snoring quietly. What he wouldn't give to be able to listen to that sound in a slightly less precarious situation.

Only thirteen-hundred-seventy-five miles to go.

Chapter Thirteen

Right Here, with You

Greta woke when the car veered onto the rumble strips. "Nico?"

"Sorry." He rubbed wearily at his face. "There's a truck stop a few miles up that advertises showers. If you think you're good to drive, we can switch off after. Unless the shower wakes me up."

Judging by the slow way he kept blinking, there wasn't much that was going to wake him up—at least not for long. It was probably a good thing his part of the drive had happened now since there weren't many other cars on the road. She wasn't sure if it was affection or stubbornness that had kept him going until she woke up. "I'm feeling a lot better, so it would probably be smart if you caught at least a couple hours sleep."

"Maybe."

There was no maybe about it. He was going to pass out as soon as they were back in the car with the monotony of a dark highway stretching ahead of them. If he woke up sooner than four hours later, she'd be shocked. As much as she craved his company and conversation, she wanted him alive and well a whole lot more.

He caught the exit ramp and pulled into a brightly lit area. Semis were parked in two lines that stretched along each side of the parking lot, and signs advertising gas, clean showers, and hot coffee glowed, cutting through the black of the night. Nico parked by the pumps and flipped open the glove compartment.

"What are you doing?" Greta asked.

"Grabbing the cash. Considering how bad we smell, I'm hoping we can at least buy some cheap T-shirts or something." He pulled out ten twenties and snapped the glove box shut again. "Plus, if they have internet access, I've figured out the message for Marron."

That *was* good news. And clothes would be nice. Her bikini and sarong weren't exactly made for driving, much less anything else as they went farther north. As it was, they were probably going to get some strange looks if the truck stop was busy. Greta grabbed their bag and slung it over her shoulder like a purse.

Inside, the building was blindingly bright...and completely empty. "Apparently, even truckers sleep at three in the morning."

"Everyone but us, Trouble. Everyone but us." Nico took her hand, gave it a squeeze, and led the way to a rack of clothes. He picked up a shirt and scowled. "We really should have shopped in Florida. I hate the Hawks."

Greta laughed, picking out a cheap hoodie and sweatpants in her size. "You'll either have to get over it or ride in the trunk."

He handed her some clothes, and they strode to the counter. The woman at the register had a Miley Cyrus mohawk and uneven piercings over her eyebrows. Greta wanted to reach out and twist them straight. Nico was more politic about things and said, "We need a fill-up on pump three, these, a shower rental, and the internet access code."

The woman nodded at Greta's bag. "We have free wifi if you have a laptop."

"Perfect. Thanks."

She shrugged like it was no big deal—she had no idea how many lives that simple amenity could save. "One shower or two? The rental is twelve bucks."

"One will do."

The woman made a face as she handed over a key card. "Damn it. I really wish you people would start fucking at home or a hotel or something. I don't get paid enough for this shit."

Nico handed over six twenties. "That should more than cover everything. Keep the change after she fills up." He nodded at Greta and took the bag. "I'm on the email. Then we shower."

"Sounds like a plan."

By the time she came in from fueling up the Civic and reparking, Nico was waiting for her. "Hopefully he deciphers the code."

"Hopefully." It had been hard, trusting him to take on the message, but everything Greta came up with was too complex and would trigger the notice of anyone watching. But it was done and one less thing to worry about. Now, the main priority was getting clean.

The shower room was much better than Greta expected— more like a nicer hotel bathroom than anything you'd find at a gas station. They could easily have taken separate showers and had plenty of room to wait while the other cleaned up. But judging by the way Nico started peeling her clothes off, that wasn't what he had in mind.

"I thought you were tired."

"I am." He nodded, tearing his shirt overhead. "Exhausted. But I have a sinking feeling the minute we get back to TRAIT, we aren't going to have a chance at sex for a while. All work and no play will make Nico a very frustrated boy. So, sex and a shower. And then a long nap."

Greta slid her hand over his chest muscles and down to his growing erection. There was nothing boylike about him. He was all man—all *her* man. "Someone better turn on the water, then."

In a flash, the water was on and pouring over them. They took turns scrubbing each other clean, not missing a spot but not lingering long, either. Nico took a few moments to make sure she was ready for him, but that was all. It was as if they both knew the only reason they had time to indulge in each other was because they weren't taking turns cleaning up. This wouldn't be the slow, lingering lovemaking they would hopefully share later or even the frantic neediness of their first time together. This would be hard and fast.

As soon as Nico had the condom rolled on, he backed Greta against a wall, and her knees hit a seat built into the shower. When Nico lifted her off the ground, she wrapped one leg around his waist and propped the other foot on the seat, taking some of her weight off him to give him the leverage he needed. He plunged into her, pinning her to the shower wall and thrusting with reckless abandon. Claiming her.

This was no quiet rejoicing in the fact they were both alive. This was a desperate reminder that it might not last. That the danger hadn't passed, and there was no telling what tomorrow would bring.

Greta clung to him as he rubbed against her clit, urging her toward climax.

She didn't want to come. Orgasm meant this was over, that they had to keep moving. That she might lose him.

If they could freeze time and stay here forever, they'd be together. And they'd be safe.

As much as she knew they had a job to do, for the first time in her life, she wondered if it was worth it.

According to the dashboard clock, they'd been on the road for about six hours, and Nico had slept through all of it. While there had probably been traffic during rush hour, the highway was pretty clear again now. He stretched and glanced over at Greta, thankful his concussion worries had been unfounded since he'd been in no shape to stay awake and keep an eye on her. Even exhausted, she was beautiful, the sun glinting off her hair and making it look like spun gold. "Any idea where we are?"

"Coming up on Louisville. We're about four and a half hours from TRAIT. I figured we could stop soon to eat, stretch, and change drivers, if you're up to it."

"Tired?"

"No. I just don't normally drive this much. Sitting still is not the best tool in my toolbox."

Shit. He'd forgotten about that. "We can switch now if you want."

"I'll make it another few minutes. I'm not that bad." She twisted her hands back and forth on the steering wheel. She needed to fidget. If he could have handed her a top to spin on the dashboard, he would have. Then she said, "I've been thinking while you slept." Uh oh… "What did the soldiers say to you when you were trying to stall them?"

"About us or the zombies?"

"They're not really zombies, you know, but yes, them."

"Easy name for a complex thing. Until they become a new species, how about we just go with easy?" At Greta's shrug, he said, "They were really adamant about not letting them out."

"I thought I heard you mention the problems in Florida."

He thought back to those tense moments aboard the *Kafka*, trying to remember exactly what he'd said. "I did. I accused them of letting one out."

Greta nodded, her hands so tight on the steering wheel that her knuckles turned white. "That's what I thought I heard you say. I couldn't really hear their response, though. This is important, Nico, what *exactly* did they say?"

Something had her worked in knots, and he had a feeling this wasn't some minor hiccup in a pattern. She'd figured out how all the pieces fit together. Closing his eyes, he thought back to the moment on the *Kafka*. They'd said something regarding charges against him and Greta, he'd snarked about the zombie crime spree, and they'd responded with… "'The subject in question has been eliminated.' That's what they said, verbatim."

"So they killed the one—likely our mysterious Mr. Smith." Instead of calming down, the news only seemed to make her more tense. Her jaw went tight, muscles all over her clenched in ways he feared would lead to an accident if she weren't careful.

"They blew up the *Kafka*. I think it's fair to say they killed them all."

"Nico, there were two dolphins torn apart. Two kids went missing. How many other incidents did we not find because we stopped looking once we had the pattern we needed for the mission? And how many of them came in pairs?"

His blood ran cold. "There were two zombies."

"And they killed *one*. Where's the other?"

"That's not good." Considering an out of control zombie would leave a path of destruction, he was trying to figure out how it was hiding. Or had it been captured? And if it had been captured, where was it? "There's no way they could have gotten one back on the ship, could they?"

Greta shrugged. "We didn't exactly get a chance to examine the entire place, much less where the subjects were being kept, but I don't think they did or they would have said that. We have to go on the assumption that one is still alive and on the loose or, potentially worse, in custody."

She'd done this while he'd been passed out—pieced together things to discover yet another horrible possibility. Could she even shut it off when she slept? Or did her brain force her to dream about patterns and the worst of human behavior? "Anything else I should know?"

"Yes, I—"

Suddenly, the Civic lurched forward. Twisting around, Nico watched as a hauntingly familiar black Suburban with heavily tinted windows slowed, pulling away from them, then sped up once more. It was the same damn one that had been watching their apartments, he would have laid money on it.

"Shit. We have company." The SUV hit them again, harder this time, and it didn't have a single scratch on it. Nico knew those vehicles, he'd read about them—clandestine street-legal tanks is what they were. Funded by the government for purposes just like this—except they were supposed to be used on the *bad guys*. "That fucker's armored, too. We aren't going to be able to take much of this, Greta."

"Right." As they crested an overpass, she pressed her foot on the accelerator, swerving into the other lane before the Suburban could hit them again, then she braked hard. "Grab the weapons and hold on!"

Shortly past the bottom of the overpass, she jerked the wheel to the right, throwing them into the ditch. Airbags deployed on impact, slamming into their faces, and as soon as Nico was able to fight free from his, he rolled out the door and onto the ground. Greta joined him before he had a chance to try to help. She reached out, and he slapped her Glock into her waiting hand. "High ground?"

She nodded. "If we can manage it before they back up."

Already, the Suburban was on the shoulder, its reverse lights on. Nico laced his fingers and gave Greta a boost onto the Civic's hood. Planting his foot on the tire, he grabbed the doorframe and yanked himself up. Greta was scrambling up the side of the ditch farthest from the road, and he joined her a few seconds later. They lay on the ground, waiting. It didn't take long before the cold started leeching through the minimal coverage of their new sweats. It might have been mild enough in Atlanta, but this far north, the weather remembered it was November. "How many do you think there are?"

"Logic says at least two. What I'm trying to figure out is how they found us."

"It probably wasn't so much they found us as they found the boat and knew we had to go somewhere." Had they been smart, they would have taken a less direct route back to TRAIT, but speed had mattered as much as secrecy.

The SUV stopped not far from the wrecked Civic, and the instant the door opened, Nico shoved Greta's head down. It wasn't like they were hidden exactly, but at least they weren't visible like it was some fucked-up game of Whack-an-Agent. Nico held his breath and counted as doors slammed. One. Two. Three. At least three people.

He raised three fingers, and Greta shook her head, reaching over to lift a fourth.

Right. Even numbers. She'd taught him once that people naturally gravitated toward even numbers. It was the reason for terms like "third wheel." Odd numbers tended to breed dissent as someone was always left as a swing vote. It wasn't a guarantee, but in this case, better safe than sorry, so he nodded.

He mouthed a countdown. "Three, two, one."

As a team, they rose from the brush and opened fire. There *were* four, just as her pattern predicted. He and Greta each took out one, surprise and the high ground working for them. The other two shot back. The Glock bucked in his hand as he squeezed the trigger. The first shot missed completely, and Nico jerked as fire grazed his ear. Too close. The next bullet caught his target in the shoulder, spinning him around. One last squeeze, and the assailant wasn't going to cause any more trouble. Ever.

He hadn't been able to watch Greta, but all four men were down, and the only blood on their side was the graze on his ear. Nico spun toward the Suburban, but no one moved there. Clearly, the patterns had fallen in their favor this time.

"Are you okay?" he asked, wanting to be absolutely sure before they moved.

"You're the one bleeding." She pushed to her feet and held out a hand for him.

He took it gratefully. "Here's hoping they have a first-aid kit in their vehicle. The Civic's out of commission."

"That would be helpful." She gazed at the mess around them. "I'd say we should move the bodies, but I don't think we have time. Considering the cars that drove by during all of this, the authorities will be here any minute."

Leaving dead bodies in their wake wasn't standard operating procedure at TRAIT. Then again, nothing about this mission had been. "Let's grab their IDs and weapons for prints just in case. Then we take their ride and get the hell out of here."

Greta nodded, already sliding onto the Civic's roof. She reached into the car and grabbed their bag, then promptly walked to the first of the men she'd shot. Nico shook his head. He wished he could shut off his emotions like that, detach himself. Instead, his gut wrenched, wondering who the men were, if they had wives, families…

One of them was still alive. He wouldn't make it, even if EMTs got there in the next minute. Blood was running a trail from his lips and his eyes rolled. This time, Nico squeezing the trigger was a mercy. He grabbed the man's wallet and gun, then walked toward the SUV.

Once upon a time, he'd thought being a spy would be all James Bond. Instead it was the *X-Files* and blood. Too much blood. He sighed at Greta as he grabbed the handle of the driver's door. "Let's get the hell out of here."

He jerked open the door, and a man lunged at him. Nico flew backward, his head crashing against the concrete. *The driver. There were five. How the hell did we miss the driver?* His head swam as it hit the road again.

Then there was a different sort of crash, and the man collapsed on top of him. An angel with a big black Glock stood there, the sun casting a halo around her blond hair.

She's so beautiful, and she's mine.

And then she disappeared as the circle of blackness closed around her.

Chapter Fourteen

IF YOU ONLY KNEW

Greta rushed forward and rolled the driver off Nico. He wasn't moving. She leaned in close, ear to his mouth, fingers to his neck. He was breathing, and his pulse was steady. Cops and emergency vehicles would be on the scene soon, but in this case, that was the worst possible news.

The men they'd killed were military. She was an agent of an organization most people didn't know about, and she wasn't supposed to flash her badge. There was no way of knowing if whoever was in charge of these people would find Nico in a hospital and finish him off there.

How had she been so stupid? So cocky? Even numbers was normal, but not an absolute. Only three doors had shut. She should have considered a driver laying in wait for them, but they'd been so damn tired that she'd just been counting her lucky stars they'd made it out of the firefight relatively unscathed.

They weren't now. Nico was injured and unconscious, and

she couldn't lift him.

Trying to control her breathing, she analyzed the situation. She needed a speedy resolution, and she needed people not to be deterred by dead bodies. Thankfully the driver was a smaller man. She shoved at his body until it was mostly under the SUV. The other visible corpses she rolled into the ditch. Then she stepped out onto the road, and the instant a vehicle crested the overpass, she started waving her arms.

The car immediately slowed and pulled over in front of the Suburban. Good. Most of the bodies were well out of view. While the man behind the wheel unbuckled, Greta threw their things in the front of the SUV and flipped all the rear seats down.

"Do you need me to call nine-one-one?" the burly man asked, rubbing at his beard and gaping at Nico's still form.

Greta yanked the Glock from her waistband and leveled it at him. "No. I need you to pick him up and put him back here. Now."

"Lady, if you're trying to kill him, a gunshot would be kinder."

"I'm trying to save him. Unless you want to need saving as well, you will pick him up and put him in the back."

"You aren't going to shoot me."

She had to suck in a breath and remind herself that she was female and thin. People underestimated her without a thought. Always had. Always would. "I've already shot three men today. Don't make it four. Now pick up my partner and get him in this damned SUV."

The guy looked down at Nico, and he must have caught sight of part of the driver's body poking out because he paled. "You aren't kidding."

"I'm not, and I'm running out of time." Why wasn't he moving? Why...?

Nico reached up a shaking hand, grabbed the guy's pant

leg and said, his voice taking on the deeper tone he used to compel people, "Buddy, trust me when I say you want to put me where she said and then drive off and forget all about us."

His hand fell again, but the man blinked. Then he blinked again. Finally, without another word, he knelt down, picked Nico up, and carried him to the back of the SUV. Clearly part of him wanted to help. Wanted to do whatever it would take to get out of this entire situation. And Nico had woken long enough to nudge him toward that decision.

Greta stepped back, her gun still trained on him until Nico was inside and the door was shut. "Now go. Just…go."

She had to wait until he got out of her way before she could risk lowering the gun. She might have been willing to shoot him, but in hand-to-hand combat, there was a chance a man of his size would still beat her years of training. As soon as he was past the SUV and headed to his own car, she raced to the driver's side, climbed in, and wheeled onto the highway, the tires bumping over the dead body beneath them. She tore off down the road, desperate to get as much distance between them and the scene of the crime as possible.

Desperate to get Nico to safety. And safety meant TRAIT. At least she hoped it did.

"Trouble?" Nico's eyes fluttered open, and he found himself staring at the headliner of what had to be their pilfered Suburban.

"Don't move."

"Too late." He pushed himself to sitting, hated himself as his head swam from the movement, then carefully slid over the center console and into the passenger seat.

Greta glared at him. "You could have a concussion or worse."

"Then you shouldn't have moved me in the first place. This seat is more comfortable than back there." He yanked on the seat belt and buckled it. "Plus, I'm restrained in case of another crash. Though I hope like hell they have a trash can or something in here, because I'm pretty sure I'm going to lose what's left of my last meal any second."

"They'd need a tank or a chopper with missiles to take down this thing." She glanced his way, worry in her eyes. "And there's a trash bag by your feet." When he winced reaching for it, she handed it over, her fingers brushing his. "Just...try to stay still."

The bit about the missiles was true enough. She was white-knuckling the wheel again, though—and that *wasn't* so good. "Are you sure you're okay to keep driving?"

"We're thirty minutes out. I'm fine."

It might not have been the driving, but something was definitely wrong. "Hey, I'm okay. Bumped and bruised and my ear is probably a mess, but I'm alive."

"I know." She shook her head as if realizing how cold her response sounded. "I'm sorry. I *am* glad you're alive. Incredibly glad, but if I'm right... Well, let's just hope I'm not right."

And that was about the least helpful thing she could have said. Nico popped open the glove compartment and prayed for some ibuprofen. His head was pounding, and trying to talk to Greta like this wasn't helping. Finally he found a bottle and popped the lid, pouring two into his hand. After a second's hesitation, he added two more.

"There's a water bottle in the console."

Grateful he wouldn't have to choke them down dry, he tossed the pills in his mouth, uncapped the water, and took a long swallow. After a couple minutes of silence, he said, "So what am I supposed to hope you're wrong about exactly?"

"Patterns. Patterns and patterns and patterns, and they all

point to the same thing."

"And that is?"

"TRAIT has been set up to take the fall for something."

Nico opened and closed his mouth several times as he tried to process her words. Whatever she'd put together in her head, he couldn't grasp it, not even knowing the outcome. "How the hell do you figure that?"

He wanted to reach out and smooth the worry lines from her face, but the instant he moved, he decided his body had other plans—namely to lean against the seatback and stay as still as possible—and it was in his best interest to listen to it.

Greta blew out a long, slow breath. "I've been an agent for five years, and TRAIT had existed for several years before I joined the ranks. In all that time, we've been a secret. We've been *so* secret that, as far as I always understood, only the President, the former President—who signed off on the agency's formation—and Secretary of Defense Rickards knew about us."

"Wait. Wasn't there a different SoD before?" Nico tried to think back to the previous administration. Usually new executives brought in new cabinet members.

"There was supposed to be a new one this time around—a friend of President Anders' from his navy days. He died in a car accident prior to taking his seat. President Anders was so grief-stricken, he pushed Rickards through as a known entity rather than looking for someone new who would have to be vetted prior to congressional confirmation."

"Oh." That made sense, and he vaguely recalled hearing about it back in high school.

"That was then, though. In the past couple years, it's like we're not a secret anymore. We've been announced to an FBI agent, a senator, a senator's kid, the attorney general, several secret service operatives… The key thing about being a super-secret secret agency is that no one is supposed to know we exist. Now, it isn't like the whole world knows, but we've been yanked out of the closet as far as DC is concerned. It doesn't make sense."

"Unless someone wants people to know who we are."

"And what we do." Greta's breath shuddered as she inhaled. There was obviously more to be said, but she was having a hard time with it right now. "Just rest. I don't want to have to explain this twice, and we'll be in the office in a few minutes."

That was easier said than done. Rest was for people who weren't starting to see all of Greta's infernal patterns. It was for people who saw trees instead of the forest.

And this was shaping up to be one dark and ugly forest.

G reta pounded on the garage door until Finn opened it. "What the fuck… Greta? Are you okay?"

"I'm fine. Nico's not. We need a wheelchair and someone to dump this SUV." She waited for him to argue with her the way he often argued with Jodi. Instead, he set his jaw, nodded, and took off at a run.

She sagged against the doorway, holding it open for Finn without losing line of sight with Nico. He'd agreed to wait for a ride, but as much as she loved him, she didn't trust him not to be foolhardy about this. Jodi dashed from the garage into the main building, and Finn rushed back with the wheelchair.

"Never thought we'd use this thing again after Sara broke her leg. Hold the door, and I'll get him. Jodi's grabbing people to get rid of the…holy shit, is that an up-armored Suburban?" Finn paused a couple feet out the door.

"Yes, and it might have a tracking device in it. Get Nico out, please."

A minute later, they were wheeling toward Marron's

office. "Slow down, Trouble. You're making my head spin, and I was really proud of myself for not puking on the drive."

"We're almost there."

"Which means slowing down only adds a few seconds." He grabbed the sides of his head and groaned as she wheeled around a corner.

Maybe she was going too fast. She slowed down, but then people started crowding, asking what happened. Marron actually came out of his office, shooed everyone else away, and took over pushing duty. As soon as he shut the door behind them, he pointed Greta to a chair and said, "Talk."

She told him about the mission, about the zombies, about Attorney General Whiddon, about the men in the boat, and their flight back to TRAIT. "I would have called, but I was hoping they thought we were dead, and there was concern that they'd infiltrated here. Did you get the email we sent?"

Marron arched a brow at her. "I don't know whose insane idea Rick-rolling me in an email was, but yes I got it. Considering I know damn well the Seattle Soldiers isn't an NFL team, I looked at it a second time and decoded that hot mess. 'Assumed dead. Defense created super-soldiers. Fail not a raccoon.' Did I miss anything?"

Greta shook her head, but Nico answered. "The code was my idea. It was the best I could come up with on short notice that would likely make it past whoever or whatever they have watching the office."

"It was a decent plan, though I almost deleted it as spam. But clearly, they haven't assumed you dead, and if Whiddon was on that ship…" He scrubbed at his face. "Please tell me you have more than this, because right now we have no evidence of an experiment that may or may not have been government sanctioned. And we already killed the damn raccoon."

"Oh. We have evidence." Greta dug in the bag, looking

for the drive they'd rescued from her wetsuit.

Nico spoke up again. "As far as more, tell me if you've heard this one… A telekinetic and a zombie walk into a bar with nerve gas and a cursed painting."

Marron's eyes narrowed at Nico, and he paid no attention at all as Greta laid the drive on his desk. "What are you getting at?"

"Conspiracy theory, only it's not really a theory so much as an inevitability."

Greta couldn't help the ghost of a smile from forming on her lips. He'd figured it out. Somehow, her crazy, wonderful partner had figured out how her brain worked. She sat down and, though she knew she'd have to explain further, said, "The short version goes like this: because a diversion was necessary to keep anyone from figuring out what was going on, Whiddon was used as a scapegoat. Now TRAIT is about to become one, too. Secretary Rickards is going to burn this place to the ground…after he kills the president and everyone who comes before him in the line of succession."

Silence descended on the office, and Marron's face turned nearly as gray as his decor. "What?"

This was going to be a hard sell, but if they didn't make him believe, they were all doomed. "He probably hatched the plan long before he met you."

"What do you mean *met me*?"

Josh Marron was a lot of things, but stupid wasn't among them. She needed to start at the beginning and spell things out slowly. "Boss, you like to forget that what I do doesn't just apply to the outside world. I deciphered TRAIT after being here a week. We aren't like the FBI or CIA. The entirety of TRAIT is housed in this one building, and you were the first agent. Something happened that drove you from your old assignment—my guess is someone died." Greta tipped her head toward the picture on his desk. "Probably her."

Before she got another word out, Marron clenched his jaw and tipped the frame down until it lay flat on his desk.

It didn't matter right now, only the path from that moment to this one did. "You wanted something you could control, something outside of the bureaucracy. Rickards found you and groomed you to be the perfect head of his new agency. You were a nonconformist, but not a renegade—the perfect man to lead a merry bunch of misfits into the breach."

"Your point, Gallagher?"

Nico stepped in again, clearly trying to diffuse some of Marron's irritation at her announcement. "Her point is that he built this agency, fully intending to destroy it when the time came. That's why you never had a decent budget. That's why as he got closer to his endgame, he was tightening the purse strings even more. That's what he's going to plant as your motive for turning all of us against the government. That's going to be the motive you supposedly had when you use all TRAIT's recent acquisitions to kill off the top people in our government."

Marron shook his head. "This makes no sense. How the hell did you come up with this ridiculous idea that he wants to take over the government by force?"

Greta blew out a slow breath, trying to calm herself now that they were reaching the end of the explanation. "The raccoon. When I pinpointed Aurora Heights as a hotspot, it was because of activity surrounding the president and every single one of the first five people in the line of succession. I didn't look further down the line because I thought six high-ranking officials was cause enough for concern. All of them had security worries. Defenses were being tested for weakness. And the pattern led to Aurora Heights…where Secretary Rickards makes his home. It wasn't a raccoon we should have put down that day. It was a snake."

"If I believe this theory, how the hell is he supposed to

take out the top six people in the government and manage to blame us for it?"

Desperate for something to cling to, something to settle her racing nerves, she reached out and wrapped her fingers in Nico's. He turned toward her and gave an encouraging smile. He believed in her. In his heart, he *knew* she was right. More than that, he knew it because he'd pieced it together, too. Their parents had been wrong about both of them. She wasn't crazy, and he wasn't useless—together they were unstoppable.

Greta returned her focus to Marron. He had to believe her, too. There simply wasn't any other option at this point. "Think about it, sir. Rickards was furious about that stupid painting getting destroyed. Why? Because he couldn't *use it*. He has Izzy Carrington, who can kill from a distance. He has Takamaki's nerve gas. And, as far as we can tell, he has a super-soldier zombie to get up close and personal. *And now TRAIT is connected to all of it.*"

She let the truth sink in for a minute. "He's planning to throw us under the bus, take over the government, and then impose martial law using the argument that the intelligence community clearly can't be trusted. No one will stand up to him, not if they think we're turning against them and we have the kind of weapons he'll put on display. Rickards doesn't plan to just become president—he'll turn the United States of America into a dictatorship. And the people will let him do it."

Chapter Fifteen

BETTER THAN I KNOW MYSELF

TRAIT was a flurry of activity like Greta had never seen before. Marron had everyone on this, and any concerns about keeping quiet had gone out the window. Well, they'd gone out the window right after he put anyone he hadn't brought in personally on administrative leave.

Though they had a pretty good handle on the hows—namely the nerve gas they'd stopped Takamaki from selling a couple years ago, Senator Carrington's telekinetic daughter who Rickards had put in "protective custody," and whichever zombified super-soldier was on the payroll—they still had to figure out when and where Rickards intended to strike. While others were churning through data, building tech, and forming contingencies for the main plan they didn't have yet, Nico and Greta were pouring through the information from the *Kafka's* computer.

Nico rubbed at his forehead. "I still think it would be easier to hire a hit on Rickards and just be done with it."

"Last resort." As much as she wanted this over, she wanted it done right. Or as right as they could. Having to stay under the radar meant they were officially keeping things nice and quiet. Though Cal had gone out of his way to weave a data trail that made it look like the President and Vice President were in danger, so they were likely under increased guard.

Greta stretched, and her spine cracked in three places. The long hours on the road had been worse for her than any amount of time at her computers. "If we kill him, he dies a hero, and TRAIT potentially goes down as the bad guy. We can prove he signed off on the missions that snagged all the weapons, but we can't prove he had anything to do with the *Kafka*. And we don't know what he did with Izzy Carrington or the gas from the Takamaki incident. It's possible the paperwork on his end says we have all of it."

"Yeah, and other than him signing off on the missions, there's no logical connection between them. To the outside world, it'll look like we were the bad guys—doing exactly what he's going to try to throw us under the bus for anyway."

"Besides, if he's planning to take out the people in front of him in the line of succession soon, there's the distinct possibility he would have his plan in play before we could neutralize him."

"I know. I get it. I just don't like it. And these videos are making it really hard to think about dinner. Much less the alone time I hoped we would get after dinner."

"You have a concussion. The most you're getting for a couple days is cuddling."

"Trouble, you sure know how to ruin a guy's day, you know that?"

"If I ruined it more than you almost dying, we need to discuss your priorities." She glanced at him quickly, taking in the way stubble shadowed his jaw, and let out a sigh that she'd have called content under better circumstances. "Though I will promise you some alone time as soon as the doctor okays it."

"And that is the way to get me to obey every single doctor's order right there."

"Good. Now let's finish these damn videos."

They were watching straight through all of them, hoping for some slip where the experiments could be connected to Rickards. Nothing. There had been no mention of who authorized the experiments, who funded the building of the ship, where the test volunteers came from.

Nico sighed. "One would think the fact that the subjects are all military would be enough since that falls under Rickards' purview."

There had been a list. All were in the military or had been, all were young, all unmarried, most orphans without any family. They'd been cherry-picked for their drive to succeed and the likelihood that no one would notice if they went missing. "It's circumstantial at best, and the more evidence we have, the better our chances of not going down with him. Last video."

Greta opened the file and pressed play, hoping this would give them something.

Dr. Brougham appeared on screen again. Haggard, with at least a week's beard growth and rumpled clothes. "May first, 2014. Mayday. Mayday." He gave a manic laugh. The man must have been going crazy, trapped on the ship with volunteers he'd turned into monsters. "We've moved all but two subjects into the hold. Both remaining subjects seem calm, much more than any of the others, so we're going to attempt to bring them up, one at a time, and gather what data we can. Still waiting on confirmation of the kill orders I requested. I'd prefer to have this taken care of prior to leaving the vessel. We may be in the middle of nowhere, but it is possible someone could stumble on the ship."

The doctor's head shot up, and his eyes went wide. "Troy. I thought Martin was escorting you."

"Marty's dealing with Scott right now, so I offered to visit you solo."

Confusion was writ in broad strokes on Dr. Brougham's face—confusion and a hint of fear. "How are you feeling? Any headaches? Nausea?" He swallowed hard. "Extreme hunger?" The other voice stayed off screen, but the doctor's reactions made it clear he was speaking to one of the two remaining subjects.

"Mild seasickness. I could really go for a day on the beach with a pig roast or something, but that was true every day before the study, too." Troy laughed.

The answer seemed to temper Dr. Brougham's reaction. "You're faring well, then. Why don't you hop up on the exam table, and I'll get your vitals." A muffled sound off camera had him jerking his head around. "What was that?"

Troy stepped behind him, only his torso visible due to the camera angle. His hands were clenched in tight fists by his side. "You forgot one important thing in your questions, Doc."

Dr. Brougham's gaze shifted back to the computer, and he frowned—likely examining whatever form he'd been filling out with Troy's answers. "I did?"

"Yeah. You forgot to ask me how hard it was to control the urge to kill you all." Troy's hands sandwiched the doctor's head and twisted, hard. The body sagged in the chair, but Troy didn't let go, he twisted Brougham's head until the skin and muscle tore. Then he yanked, and the body crumbled to the floor, the decapitated head still in Troy's hands. "It was pretty fucking easy, as long as I knew I'd get to do it eventually."

He tossed the head away, shoved the chair, and squatted down to camera height. "Congratulations, sir, the experiment was a rousing success. My puppy, Scott, and I will be leaving the ship as soon as we have a bite to eat. See you shoreside.

And you should probably come prepared to put that bulldog down. I've kind of grown fond of him since January, and I'd rather not do it myself. All other loose ends shall be promptly tied."

The video ended, pausing on Troy's face.

Greta stared at the screen, transfixed. "He's not a mindless zombie."

"Nope. He ripped that guy's head off…just ripped it right off." It didn't help that Nico seemed as shocked as she was. The experiment being a failure was scary enough. Knowing it had succeeded was terrifying.

"Names. We need names and all the intel we can gather."

A rapping sounded at the door and Jodi stepped inside the office, sweeping back her unruly red hair. "Hey, did you want Taser capabilities on that… Why are you watching videos of Agent Anderson?"

"Who?" Greta asked.

"Anderson. He was assigned to Senator Carrington's house. In fact, he was the one that let us inside and was the last one I talked to before Finn rushed me back to TRAIT because of the threats."

Greta snapped to the intake list from Brougham's computer.

Troy Anderson. 26. Former army intelligence. Approved for secret service.

Greta could barely breathe as she said, "And that's how you kill a president."

It had taken another full day before they got everything they needed. Cal hacked into Rickards' home network and poked around his email, eventually calling Trevor in to translate an email chain regarding a fund-raiser gala coming up on the weekend.

From there, Marissa used all the skills she'd learned as the child of con artists to snag TRAIT passes to the event as well as a detailed layout diagram. She was working with Finn on an infiltration plan while he helped Jodi build the tech.

Nico frowned at the activity. "I feel useless."

"Without us, there'd be no big mission. Without us, by this time next week, we'd all be in jail." Greta shrugged. "We aren't useless. Now come and help me with this."

Shaking off the frustration brought on by doing so much in the last few days to being stuck in the wheelchair yesterday to feeling unnecessary today, Nico sank into the chair next to Greta. "You mean we actually have a job to do?"

"Yes, just not an assigned one. We need to figure out how Rickards is likely to use the resources in his control. We don't have enough to just arrest him, so we have to catch him in the act, and that means"—she ticked off items on her fingers—"preventing the release of the gas, and neutralizing both Anderson and Senator Carrington's daughter. All of that, preferably without alerting the SoD to our presence there."

"That still isn't getting Rickards behind bars. He'll just start over." The whole thing sucked balls. Without the support of the Department of Defense, TRAIT was done for. So if they foiled the plot but didn't get Rickards in the process, all of this was over. The band would be breaking up, and there'd be no way to stop it. Nico tossed impotence on top of all the other negative emotions he had going on today.

At least he had Greta.

She smiled at him. "Well, that's the other part of what we're doing. I want to try to predict his behavioral patterns enough to either get him in the line of fire if things go badly or get him to say something stupid around the wrong people. So, help me. What do we know about him?"

People. That was one thing Nico did know. He glared at

the photo of Rickards that Greta had pulled up on one of the monitors, wishing it was the man in person instead. *Soon, you piece of shit.* "Get ready to type until your fingers bleed. For starters…"

N ico dragged a finger inside his collar in a vain attempt to loosen it. No one had said monkey suits were required for this gig. Greta strode up on four-inch heels and tugged on the skirt of her dress like she was trying to keep the slit from gaping open. "Trade you?" she asked.

"Nope. No matter how sexy you might look in a tux, I'm kind of enjoying the view." He crooked his elbow. "Shall we?"

Greta took his arm and blew out a breath. Then she moved her jaw in the way that activated her comm device. "We're in position."

Nico listened as everyone else checked in. While they had a decent-sized team outside the gala, inside their force was significantly smaller. Jodi and Finn—whose job it was to get to Izzy Carrington—Marron, and the two of them. Cal, Marissa, and Trevor were on a hunt for the nerve gas. If and when they found and disarmed the device, they'd change clothes and come inside, but there was no guarantee of their presence.

Everyone was good to go. Marron was already inside, so Nico led Greta to the entrance and handed over their passes. After a security sweep came up clean—it obviously hadn't detected the ceramic blades they had hidden—they were allowed inside. The gala was a sea of bodies in dresses and tuxedos. How the hell were they supposed to find Rickards *or* Anderson?

Marron's voice came over the comm, "Anderson is assigned to the president. Not sure if that means he's backup in case Carrington gets cold feet or if he has some other role.

We need eyes on him—now."

"Got it," Greta said.

A few seconds later, Finn announced, "We spoke to the Carringtons. We're removing the senator and Izzy now. Apparently the carrot for getting her to kill someone was a threat against her father's life. We're keeping them both with us to ensure his safety, and Izzy agreed to direct us to the compound where she was being held. There's likely proof there, linking her abduction and the threat to Rickards."

"Good job, but be careful. Who knows what other measures he may have taken," Marron said. "If you find evidence, get back here and get it to the president. The sooner he knows about the snake in his cabinet, the better off we'll all be."

Great, two agents heading out the door, and he and Greta were on zombie duty. What they really needed was more bodies in here, not fewer. "I wonder how they're faring on the nerve gas?"

An irritated female voice crackled over the comm. "They're faring fine. We've been searching all the nooks and crannies indicated for a whopping ten minutes. Nothing yet. Keep your freaking panties on."

Nico winced. "Sorry, Marissa." He switched the voice part of his comm off. "I really need to figure out how to make your bestie like me."

"She likes *you* fine," Greta corrected, squeezing his arm. "She also volunteered to personally sneak into Rickards' office and slip a blade between his ribs. TRAIT is pretty much the only home Marissa has ever known. She's taking this whole thing as a personal attack."

The problem was he was taking it the same way. Everyone at TRAIT fit there, even if they didn't fit anywhere else in the world. Rickards had built a place like that, only to destroy it without a thought. Nico agreed with Marissa—though he'd prefer the Secretary of Defense suffer a slow, torturous death to the quick one she'd intended.

Near the dais now, Nico barely recognized Anderson as the man from the video. But black suit and stiff posture aside, it was definitely him. He leaned toward Greta. "To the president's right."

Greta nodded, then spoke into her comm, "Eyes on target. When should we engage?"

Marissa chimed in right after. "I've got the box. Location Foxtrot. On a timer—fifteen minutes. Probably remote detonator, too. It's a mess in here, guys. To me, ASAP. Will update as something changes."

Shit. No backup anytime soon.

"Stay on task and get that gas dealt with. Then we're down to only one threat. One big threat, but still one threat." Marron paused for a second. "Damn it. Rickards caught sight of me. He's headed this way. Going off mic."

Which meant the zombie super-soldier was all on him and Greta. She glanced his way. "Too bad we probably can't get him to talk, huh?"

"Yeah." Rickards would if properly motivated, but not Anderson. Based on what they knew of Troy Anderson, proper motivation for him was killing, which wasn't an option.

Nico scowled at Anderson. Then he blinked.

They're already taking bets on who'll get the title of Captain America.

This might not have been a comic book, but if the rules applied at all, the changes to Anderson would only increase what was already there. Which meant predictability and patterns—his favorite woman's specialty. Everything started lining up in his head like puzzle pieces just waiting to be put into place. Too bad in order to move the one he could actually control, it meant leaving the other to Greta.

It meant leaving her to potentially get killed.

Chapter Sixteen

NOTHING TO DO WITH LOVE

Greta was watching Anderson watch the president when Nico grabbed her. "I have a plan, but I have to go to Rickards. Can you handle Anderson?"

"Can I handle the super-soldier who ripped a man's head off?"

"Never mind. It's stupid. Marron will figure something out." Nico wrapped an arm around her waist and squeezed.

It was the squeeze that did it. Nico wasn't trying to comfort her fears but his own, which meant he'd figured out something that would likely work, but it meant leaving her alone with Anderson. And that didn't even take into account the nerve gas set to be released in less than fifteen minutes—probably less than fourteen now. They didn't have time for hesitation or fear. They were TRAIT, and they needed to act like the best of the best, no matter what Rickards had intended them to be. She twisted in his embrace and brushed a kiss over his mouth. "Go. I've got this."

"Are you sure?"

"Of course." *Not at all.*

"Just remember everything you learned about him. He's still the same guy underneath all the extra oomph. Use it if you have to; stay the hell away from him if you can, though."

The look in his eyes was so earnest, so hopeful, it made her feel terrible for what she was about to do. One of the things she'd learned from her friendship with Marissa was because she wasn't a great liar, she shouldn't do it very often. That way, when she did, no one would expect it. Greta forced a smile and nodded. "I can definitely do that."

Nico pressed his lips briefly to her forehead and then walked away. His voice came through her comm unit. "Marron, I'm on my way to you. If you have a way to start recording, do it now."

With him wending his way through a sea of power-players, Greta was alone with a super-soldier who had a propensity for decapitation. Of course, he also had a thing for blondes. She could use that.

What else *had* they learned? Army intelligence with a pristine record, but he didn't re-up after his tour. Instead he'd used that to segue into the secret service, with a brief stop at Secretary Rickards' Ship of Crazypants. Prior to the army, he'd been an athlete in high school. Good enough to make a college team but not good enough for a scholarship to play.

Glory days were in high school, and he likes blondes.

Too bad using any of that would mean getting close to him. And she failed at interpersonal communication.

If Marissa were here, she could do it without a second thought, but she was playing diffuse-the-bomb. And she wasn't blonde right now.

Anderson shifted his stance. He wasn't watching the president anymore; his eyes were on the clock, and his hands were clenched into fists. Just like they had been before he'd killed Brougham.

Shit. He was going to make a move, and soon.

What did they have left? Twelve minutes? Ten? She had to do something…now.

Greta switched her comm to single-channel mode. "Marissa, leave the bomb to the guys. I need your help."

Finding Marron wasn't hard. Nico had seen where he'd been stationed on entering, and he hadn't moved far. Plus, the guy tended to command a room whether he meant to or not. He was standing off in a corner with Secretary Rickards, the two of them in a heated enough conversation that most people were giving them a wide berth.

Nico stepped right into the open area. "Hey, aren't you Orson Rickards?"

The man narrowed his eyes, as if trying to ID him in return. "This isn't a good time."

"When is it ever? Am I right?" He stationed himself as the third point of their triangle, out of reach but too close to ignore. It allowed Marron a little breathing room if he hadn't switched on a recording device yet. "But I heard this crazy story about a guy who was looking to assassinate the president. And it was a crap story. I mean, the plan was utter horseshit. So I told my friend, 'You know who would probably be the best at planning something like that? Someone already close to the target. A friend. A partner even.' I mean, you're connected to all of DC's power players. If you were going to kill one of them, how would you do it?"

Nico could almost see Marron registering what he was doing. Nico couldn't *force* someone to give up info, but Rickards was the kind of guy who liked to brag. Even if his plan was completely successful, he'd need someone to tell his tale to. And if he wanted to tell, Nico could make that happen.

"Agent Tancredi, I know damn well who you are and what you're doing. So why don't you walk away before you hurt yourself?"

Or maybe not.

But the real question was how *much* did he know about Nico?

"Orson, can I call you Orson? Actually, how about O? Like Oprah." A little distraction never hurt anyone…except the target. "Actually that sounds dirty. Rickards it is. So, anyway, you know I'm a TRAIT agent, but what you don't know is this is a stepping stone for me." *Spin, spin, spin…* and pray Marron didn't think it was truth in the end. "What I learned in the army and my time here is you're really the guy I want to work for. I want to be your right hand." *Feed his ego. Make him feel powerful.* Nico pushed every ounce of conviction into his voice that he could muster. "What do I have to do to make that happen?"

Rickards narrowed his eyes for a long moment and then smiled. "Simple. Kill your current boss."

Damn it. That really hadn't been what he'd had in mind. "Now?"

"Naturally."

Looking around, Nico laughed. "I want to work for you, not go to prison for you. This many witnesses, there's no way I walk out of this a free man." Actually, if he really wanted to do it, it wouldn't be hard. Marron was cornered, rather literally, and death by ceramic knife wouldn't involve any sound as long as he was quick about it.

"Trust me when I say that in a few moments, no one is going to be worried about him."

The bomb. They probably had less than ten minutes by now, but this was what Nico had been hoping for. He just had to play it right. "What do you mean?"

Rickards snorted. "You TRAIT people just don't get it, do you? I control you. I control this building. Humanity will never learn from its mistakes. Neither, it seems, will TRAIT. Now either kill him, or get out of my way."

Mistakes? That wasn't just a figure of speech here. It was a slam. That was how Rickards operated. He would use their mistakes against them. Make it look as if they'd done it intentionally. Nico thought back on the missions, all the missions that had led to this moment. When he saw the truth, he almost cracked his neck activating his comm. "Is there a code on the bomb?"

In front of him, Rickards rolled his eyes. "What bomb?"

In his ear, however, Cal said, "Yes, why?"

Nico hoped like hell everyone still had their ears on. "Finn, Jodi, we need the access code you used on Senator Carrington's house when you were protecting Izzy."

The response was drowned out by a roar from Rickards. "No!"

He lunged at Nico, but Marron was on top of the man in an instant, yanking his arms behind his back. "Pretty sure that little display, along with the other evidence we've gathered should be enough to put you away for life."

Rickards scowled at them. "Enjoy it now. But you better hope your pretty little girlfriend brought an army with her." He tipped his head toward the dais, toward Greta. "Because after he takes the president down, my guy isn't going to quit until he's bathing in blood. You can't stop this. None of you can, but especially not someone as inconsequential as her."

Nico scrambled to his feet and looked back, only to find Anderson already had Greta by the arm. Rickards was right—he was too late.

"This is a horrible idea, Greta." Marissa had been saying that for a while, but Greta didn't care anymore.

"He's making a move on the president, and we have a bomb set to go off in roughly eight minutes. I either do *something* or my vote was wasted. Not to mention the fact that Anderson could really get the munchies and kill a lot of people. So help, because I have to get close to him before he gets close to President Anders, and I don't have time to keep talking to *you*."

Besides, Greta was already halfway up the steps of the dais. Anderson must have caught sight of her movement because he turned from the president and narrowed his eyes. He'd reverted in an instant from killing machine to protector. Funny that he'd worry about *her* being a threat against the man he'd been created to kill.

"You're right; we're on a countdown." Marissa went quiet for a few seconds. "I'm out of contact with the boys. I only have ears for you. As stupid as I think this is, I'll help as much as I can."

Thank goodness. She knew she couldn't get through this alone.

After nodding to the other Secret Service agent, Anderson strode toward her. "Can I help you, ma'am?"

In her ear, Marissa said, "Stop walking, pop your hip *a little*, and let the slit of your dress fall open over your thigh."

Greta really didn't want to do *that*, but she'd started this thing, she had to follow through now. She tried to follow Marissa's instructions, but when the slit fell open, she realized her hip was shifted so far she probably looked like she was trying to emulate Jessica Rabbit. Standing a little more upright helped, but Anderson was already staring at her like she was an idiot.

"Ma'am?"

"Shit," Marissa said. "He's going to make you talk. Go

with something about how you saw him and couldn't resist coming up to say hello. Feed his ego about being a big, strong man."

A big, strong man who liked to rip people's heads off. Instead of mentioning that, Greta said, "I was standing down there, waiting for the president to talk, and then all I could see was you." Truth worked better for her than Marissa's games, but at least she had her coach handy in case things went south. "I've always wondered what it took to be a Secret Service agent."

"That's not feeding his ego…"

But it seemed to work well enough. Anderson hadn't lost his assertive posture, but he was moving closer to her, and he was smiling. Had Greta not known what he was, what he was willing to do, she might have found him attractive in an objective fashion. "I need to ask you to go back down those stairs." He laid a hand on her arm, his fingers sliding along her skin like he could memorize it. *Zombie. Nico was right. It's easier to think of him that way.* "If you want to discuss my job after the gala, we could certainly do that. But if you stay now, you're going to be a distraction…"

He was borderline charming, too. Charming zombies? Not even in the craziest fiction would anyone believe that.

Then a roar from the other side of the room made him snap his head around. Greta didn't have to look; she knew. Nico had gotten to Rickards, but he'd done it before she'd had a chance to take out Anderson, and now she was fucked.

She tried to pull away, but arms like steel wrapped around her, dragging her tight against Anderson's chest. "Who are you?" he growled in her ear.

"Help?" she said, the word barely more than a squeak.

Anderson must have thought… Well, she didn't know what he thought, but he loosened his grip on her and said, "Answer the question."

Marissa, on the other hand, said, "Use the glory days thing — distract him with that."

Lies…more lies? She was so bad at that. Bits of truth, but not the whole truth. Hadn't Marissa told her that once? "I — I was a cheerleader back in high school." Anderson grew up locally. It wasn't a stretch that someone from his high school might be here. His grip slackened a little more. "I never thought you got the recognition you deserved." Because it made no sense to her that people didn't see him for the monster that he was. "And I just wanted to get close to you."

His hands flexed against her skin. Fists. He was trying to make fists like he had before his other kill — only his hold on her got in the way. His hands skated up to her shoulders, then her neck. "You're close to me now."

How long did they have until the bomb went off now? Six minutes? Five? If they managed to stop that danger, would someone still be able to take out Anderson? Or would all of this have been for nothing?

"Greta!" Nico's voice was close, but not close enough to help.

Anderson's hands shifted again. In seconds, he'd grab her by the head and it would be over. She'd be dead, and she wouldn't even get a chance to tell Nico how she really felt.

"Not today," she whispered. Not caring who she flashed in the process, Greta reached through the slit in her skirt, grabbed her knife, and spun, sliding the blade between two of Anderson's ribs as she spun away.

His eyes went wide with shock, and blood spilled from the wound. Unfortunately, that was the only sign of injury at all. With an evil grin, he gripped the blade and pulled it free in a spray of blood. "Is that all you've got?"

"Marissa?"

Her friend's voice was in her ear. "You don't need me anymore. Kick his ass."

"On it." But she wasn't, not by a long shot. She had no weapon. Her partner was still trapped in a sea of people. *Kick ass...kick ass...* She tried to think about the movie, but channeling Hit Girl wasn't going to do a damn thing to get her through this, especially not with the way Anderson was toying with her—and her damn knife.

Other things might, though. Snapshots in her mind flashed in rapid sequence. Fabric draped behind the dais. Mics on stands near the front. Stairs. Speakers.

Anderson stopped flipping the blade, holding it in an attack grip. The time for thinking was over. She needed to play the patterns.

As he advanced, Greta dodged toward the back wall. Grabbing the edge of the fabric, she spun, and twisted it around Anderson. The move wasn't perfect by any means, but it gave her a few precious seconds to think while Nico pushed toward the stairs.

The people below had finally noticed the chaos on the stage, but Greta didn't have time for them. If they were too dumb to get out of the way, that was their fault. But there was still a bomb ticking—and not knowing about that didn't make them stupid. She glanced at the microphones, then back at Anderson, who was using her blade to slice his way free.

Greta raced to the microphone, turned it on, and said, "Get out of here, you idiots. The president is gone, don't you think maybe that means you should be, too?" Then she yanked the mic from the stand.

Anderson was free, she could feel his footsteps vibrating as he ran. Grabbing the stand, she swung the thing at him, swiping low enough to catch him at the knees. Super-soldier or not, the impact made his legs buckle. The instant they did, she jerked back on the stand, then drove it forward like a spear. It hit him in the neck, and he made a strangled sound.

He clutched his throat with one hand as he reached for his

Sig Sauer with the other. Now people screamed and started running. How much time did they have left? These people weren't going to make it.

There wasn't time for more thought because arms wrapped around her from behind. "You're under arrest for assault with intent to kill and—" The voice of the new agent staggered to a stop. "Anderson? You're okay?"

"I'll be okay once I'm covered in that little bitch's blood." Gun arm not the least bit shaky, Anderson leveled the Sig at her.

There were no more patterns. He shouldn't have been standing or talking after what she'd just done to him. Instead he had murder in his eyes and his finger on the trigger.

Before she had time to even decide how to move, Nico flew across the space, barreling into Anderson. The gun went off—and both men stayed on the ground for a moment—then Anderson started to rise again.

"No!" she screamed, flailing desperately. He couldn't be dead. He *couldn't*. It was more impossible to her than Anderson still being alive. Nico… He'd saved her, damn it, and he couldn't leave like this. Heroes didn't die this way.

The agent's arms slacked around her as his own shock at seeing Anderson rise set in. That piece of shit wasn't taking anyone else. Not if she could stop it.

Greta no longer cared about the mission, about the president, about anything else. There was only the monster before her. And Nico. He was her top, and she couldn't stop spinning. Not now, not like this.

She twisted on the agent, grabbed his weapon, and shoved him backward. Dropping to her knees, she aimed up, squeezing the trigger. The first bullet tore through the underside of Anderson's jaw, driving straight through his head. As his chin fell, she saw the blood burbling at the corner of his lips, but she didn't trust it. After all they'd seen, she couldn't.

The way he lifted his own Sig only confirmed her fears.

He is *a zombie. A heartless, soulless zombie.*

Sucking in a breath, thinking of nothing but getting to Nico, she targeted on Anderson's face and said, "Double-tap, motherfucker."

This time when the weapon bucked in her hand, she rolled away. Anderson's body fell right where she'd been, his weapon discharging as he hit. Greta stayed in firing position for a second, but he didn't rise again.

Before the other agent regained his senses and came for her, she crawled over to Nico. Blood slicked the jacket of his tux and spread along the right side of the crisp white shirt underneath. Not his heart…please, not his heart. "Nico? Nico!"

His lips quirked into a lopsided smile. "Trouble? Did I seriously just hear you channeling both *Zombieland* and Samuel L. Jackson?"

Greta could barely breathe as she clung to him. "You're alive!"

"Yeah. More or less, though my eardrums might be a little shattered. Anyone ever told you how loud you get when you're excited?"

"No, never," she whispered as she lay down next to him, needing to be close and not caring how many guns were pointed in their direction. They were getting arrested, and it didn't matter. All that mattered was they were alive. Well, that and they had enough evidence to prove their innocence. "I'm quiet right now because I'm so excited you're alive. I get loud when I get scared—especially when I'm scared the man I love just got himself shot being a hero."

"You love me?" He reached up and ran his fingers through her hair.

"I do."

"Then how about you make an honest man out of me and

say those words again after we get out of jail? But I want you to say them in front of all our friends, our fucked-up families, if necessary, and the minister of your choosing."

Was he…? "You're delirious, Nico."

"No, I'm thinking clearer than I ever have, and if I know anything, it's that in a world where zombies, telekinetics, cursed paintings, and megalomaniacal politicians exist, the most incredible thing is still that I found you. I don't want to risk losing you again. Marry me, Trouble?"

"So is this going to be our pattern? Someone has to get hurt before we admit how we feel?"

"Nah. That pattern is over the minute you say yes. Then we get to start making new patterns."

Greta laid her head on his chest and closed her eyes, shutting out the rest of the world. His heart thrummed a comforting rhythm, calm and steady. Hers didn't match it at all, not with the way it had skipped a beat then sped as if to catch up with his.

Nico was right…again. This was the end of one story and the beginning of something else, something they could share together. "Yes. For you, my answer will always be yes. That's our new pattern." And it was one she never wanted to end.

Epilogue

Marron stood, straightened his dark gray jacket, and shot Greta a very stern expression. "It's time. Are you sure you want to do this? You have a very narrow window of opportunity left to back out. It closes the minute you walk through those doors."

Smiling at her own reflection in the gilt-edged mirror, Greta sucked in a deep breath. "I've never been this sure about a mission in my career."

"I don't know how I let Nico convince me to be part of this mess," he grumbled. For once, Greta could read him without thinking about it. It might have been the smile behind the sound.

"No disrespect, but I was the one who asked you. Nico's powers of persuasion had nothing to do with it." Which was the only way she'd been comfortable with it at all. It felt like asking too much, and she hadn't wanted him to be pressured to say yes. She turned and touched him on the arm. "Thank you for doing this, sir."

"Considering I'm about to pretend to be your father,

maybe you could start calling me Josh? Or really anything other than *sir*."

"In that case, thank you, Josh." No. That wasn't going to last. He might not be her dad, but he was her boss. Once they were back at the office, she was going back to sir whether he liked it or not.

"You ready?"

Greta was about to nod when she remembered. "Oh my God. One more thing."

She lifted up the shimmering white skirt of her dress, showing off more leg than strictly recommended around one's boss, and tied her *Buffy the Vampire Slayer* top to the bow of her garter. "Something old. Now I'm ready."

"Good, because if you'd called me your something old, I was going to have to fire you."

Laughing, Greta took Marron's arm, and the doors swung wide. Rows and rows of people stood. Greta's fingers clenched, gripping tighter. Then she caught sight of Nico standing at the front of the room, and all her nerves settled.

They hadn't bothered with the pomp and circumstance of having a bridal party march up the aisle. Finn stood by Nico's side, and Marissa waited on the other. Her voice whispered in Greta's ear, "Remember to walk slowly. It's not a race; it's a procession. Also, you look beautiful, so show it off. Oh, and in case I forgot to mention it, the comm goes dark once you're up here; you're on your own for vows."

Greta's lips twitched as she fought the urge to laugh. She'd been so nervous about everything, she'd insisted on the comm just in case, but now, walking toward her soon-to-be-husband, she had no worries at all.

At the altar, Marron hugged her, and instead of planting a kiss on her cheek as planned, he whispered in her ear, "Now's your chance. Run. I'll slow him down."

This time, the giggle came out no matter how hard she

fought it. She hugged him back. "No good, old man. Even if you slow him down, I'm not Marissa. I can't run in heels."

He joined her laughter, then placed her hand in Nico's. "Never a dull moment with you two."

"That's the plan, boss," he said, grinning.

Once everyone was settled, President Anders raised his hands and started speaking, "Dearly beloved, we are gathered here today to join this man and this woman… No. That's not right. We're gathered here today to join these two heroes in the joyous sacrament of marriage. It's not a union to be entered into lightly or unadvisedly. However, these two have made doing what would be ill-advised for others into an art form. They do it to save lives and protect our futures. They do it out of dedication, trust, and a love that knows no bounds. And, even if their ways are somewhat unconventional, are those not three of the most important things a marriage needs to succeed?"

The president kept talking, but Greta stopped listening. Every ounce of her being was focused on Nico. The way his bow tie was slightly askew, crooked, just like his smile. The way the candlelight reflected in his deep brown eyes. The way he looked at her as if she were the only thing that mattered to him as well.

Then suddenly Nico was speaking. Vows. They had to do their vows.

"Greta, the very first moment I met you, my world went topsy-turvy. I couldn't tell up from down, much less from sideways. I thought I had finally figured out the path of my life, but you set me so far off course, I knew from that very moment, there was no going back. I am with you until the end, and today I'm vowing that in front of our family and friends and the damn president, so that you *never* question it. You and me—odd as everyone else might think we are—we found each other, and somehow we work. And *I* will never question that." He slid the ring on her finger—a perfect fit, just like the two of them.

Marissa nudged her in the back, and Greta said, "I might have set your world spinning, but you stabilized mine. For all the things I can see in the world, I never thought I'd see that happen. I didn't think it *could*—until you. Nicolas Tancredi, you swept into my life like a whirlwind, and I didn't know how to deal with you. I didn't think to try because I couldn't let myself believe you'd stay. But every time I said no, you said okay, but you never left. You never abandoned me. You waited. You waited for me to realize that I couldn't bear the thought of my life without you in it. And then, once we were friends, you let me learn to love you. You are the thing that keeps me steady when the world tries to knock me down. I'm sorry it took me as long as it did to recognize that. I won't forget again." Hands shaking, Greta slipped his ring on.

"With the power vested in me by the District of Columbia and the voters of this great nation, I pronounce you husband and wife—and heroes to your country. You may kiss the bride."

Their lips pressed together, sealing their future, and they parted on a blissful sigh. As President Anders introduced them as Mr. and Mrs. Nicholas Tancredi, Greta leaned close to him and whispered, "There is one more thing we have to do."

"What's that?" he whispered back.

"We need to rename my cat. I can't handle two Mr. Perfects in my life."

Acknowledgments

Last book of the series…it feels so strange knowing that. TRAIT has been a wild ride for me from the first book until this one, and there are a lot of people to thank.

Libby Murphy, for picking me out of the slush with *Gaming for Keeps*. Allison for being with me on the second book. And the amazing Karen Grove for taking on the last two books in the series, especially when I said I was done with doing them novella length. She's been incredible to work with, and I'm very proud of what we built together. Thanks for embracing my crazy and not raising a brow at the pizza boy reference.

To all the beta readers through the series (Katee, Dani, Janelle, Diane—I really hope I didn't miss anyone) as well as my "gun guys," Jesse and Ken, and Tracey and Dina who helped immensely whenever I had injury questions. You guys have no idea how messy these books would have been without your help.

To the real-life guy who inspired Nico—thanks for the stories, and I hope someday you find your Greta.

This one is dedicated to my street team, The Renegades. All too often, writing is the profession of reluctant hermits. We become trapped in our own heads with all our neuroses and fall prey to the "Oh my God, I suck" attitude all the time. That happened for me with this series more often than I care to count. Through it all, The Renegades were there with laughs and pics of hot men as encouragement. I wish I had the ability to repay all their kindness and support.

Almost finally, Agents of TRAIT wouldn't exist at all if not for Liz Pelletier, Heather Howland, and all the other awesome people at Entangled. I am incredibly blessed to be surrounded by such fantastic people and be part of such an amazing company.

The biggest thank-you, as always, goes to my family—especially my children. They put up with my crazy hours and insanity and support me no matter what. You are what make all the madness worth it. Every second. I love you.

About the Author

At a young age, Seleste deLaney discovered the trick to not being afraid of the monsters under the bed was to turn them into heroes. Since that time, she's seen enough of human monsters that she prefers to escape to fictional worlds where even the worst demons have to play by the rules and the good guys might end up battered and bruised (or dead), but they always win. And really, isn't that the way it should be?

She resides in the Detroit area with all her favorite monsters (nice ones—some are furry and the others call her Mom) and is hard at work on her next book. In those rare moments when she isn't battling terrorists, vampires, or rogue clockworks, she can be found all over the internet, where she loves to interact with readers.

Discover the **Agents of TRAIT** *series...*

GAMING FOR KEEPS
an *Agents of TRAIT* novel by Seleste deLaney

Pen Holloway's done with real-life men. Guys in game are much less drama. But when her gaming partner invites her to the year's biggest convention, Pen panics that he might be yet another jerk. Cal Burrows has the perfect job as a TRAIT spy, until an arms dealer invades his not-so-secret geek haven. Now, with the threat of mass murder looming, he's forced to choose between keeping his mission a secret and protecting the girl of his dreams. And Pen can't help but suspect Cal's hiding something...

CONNING FOR KEEPS

FIGHTING FOR KEEPS